More Daisy adventures!

☆

"Zem clever kidskies are after us."

Olaf the Russian Burglar

☆

"You're not doing any fingerprinting

with my icing sugar!"

Gabby's mum

☆

"Good afternoon everybody

and welcome!"

Daisy's headmaster

☆

"Oh no."

Daisy's teacher

www.daisyclub.co.uk

More Daisy adventures!

DAISY AND THE TROUBLE WITH LIFE

DAISY AND THE TROUBLE WITH ZOOS

DAISY AND THE TROUBLE WITH GIANTS

DAISY AND THE TROUBLE WITH KITTENS

DAISY AND THE TROUBLE WITH CHRISTMAS

DAISY AND THE TROUBLE WITH MAGGOTS

DAISY AND THE TROUBLE WITH COCONUTS

DAISY AND THE TROUBLE WITH BURGLARS

DAISY AND THE TROUBLE WITH SPORTS DAY

DAISY AND THE TROUBLE WITH PIGGY BANKS

A WINTER
DOUBLE
DAISY

A WINTER DOUBLE DAISY
A RED FOX BOOK 978 1 782 95533 7

First published in Great Britain by Red Fox,
an imprint of Random House Children's Publishers UK
A Penguin Random House Company

Penguin
Random House
UK

DAISY AND THE TROUBLE WITH BURGLARS
First published in Great Britain by Red Fox in 2013

Text copyright © Kes Gray, 2013
Cover illustration copyright © Nick Sharratt, 2013
Inside illustrations copyright © Garry Parsons, 2013
Character concept copyright © Kes Gray, 2013

DAISY AND THE TROUBLE WITH CHRISTMAS
First published in Great Britain by Red Fox in 2009

Text copyright © Kes Gray, 2009
Cover illustration copyright © Nick Sharratt, 2009
Inside illustrations copyright © Garry Parsons, 2009
Character concept copyright © Kes Gray, 2009

This edition published 2015

3 5 7 9 10 8 6 4 2

Text copyright © Kes Gray, 2015
Cover illustration copyright © Nick Sharratt, 2015
Inside illustrations copyright © Garry Parsons, 2015
Character concept copyright © Kes Gray, 2015

The right of Kes Gray, Nick Sharratt and Garry Parsons to be identified as
the author and illustrators respectively of this work has been asserted in
accordance with the Copyright, Designs and Patents Act 1988.

Set in 15/23pt Vag Rounded

RANDOM HOUSE CHILDREN'S PUBLISHERS UK
61–63 Uxbridge Road, London W5 5SA

www.**randomhousechildrens**.co.uk
www.**totallyrandombooks**.co.uk
www.**randomhouse**.co.uk

Addresses for companies within The Random House Group Limited can be found at:
www.**randomhouse**.co.uk/offices.htm

THE RANDOM HOUSE GROUP Limited Reg. No. 954009

A CIP catalogue record for this book is available from the British Library.

Penguin Random House is committed to a sustainable future for
our business, our readers and our planet. This book is made from
Forest Stewardship Council® certified paper.

MIX
Paper from
responsible sources
FSC® C018179

Printed and bound in Great Britain by Clays Ltd, St Ives plc

A WINTER DOUBLE DAISY

Daisy and the Trouble with Burglars and
Daisy and the Trouble with Christmas

BY KES GRAY

RED FOX

To Kathy,
best wishes on your retirement!

DAISY

and the **TROUBLE** with

BURGLARS

by Kes Gray

RED FOX

CHAPTER 1

The **trouble with burglars** is they are really hard to catch.

If burglars were easier to catch, then my mum would never have got told off by a policeman this evening. Or let a policeman see her in her nightie. Or had her car taken away.

Catching burglars is one of the

hardest things to do in the whole wide world. Especially if you've only got one box of icing sugar. And no fingerprinting brush. And no microscopes either. Which isn't my fault!

CHAPTER 2

I knew something exciting was happening this morning because the phone in our house rang at 6.52!

The **trouble with phone calls** is it's really hard to know what's being said unless you are one of the people who is holding the phone. Even when I sat right up close beside my mum and strained my ears really hard, I still couldn't tell what she was talking about.

Whatever was being said in the phone call was definitely, definitely, really, really interesting though. These are the words that I could hear clearly:

Aha?

Aha.

Aha.
Aha.
Aha.
Aha.
Aha.
No.
Aha.
Aha.
Aha.
Aha.
Noooo . . .
Nooooooooooo . . .
Aha.
They didn't?
Three?
In one night?

Aha.

Aha.

Aha.

Aha.

Nooooo . . . they never.

Anything valuable?

Aha.

Aha.

Aha . . .

That's terrible.

Haddock?

Haddock and cod too!

Noooo.

No.

Nooooo.

Nooooo . . .

No burglar alarm then . . . !

I bet they'll get one now.

As soon as Mum said the 'b' word,
I knew exactly what had happened.
Well, not exactly. But almost exactly.

Someone – I wasn't sure who . . .

somewhere – I wasn't sure where . . .

had . . .

for absolutely definite . . .

wait for it . . .

been burgled!

CHAPTER 3

As soon as Mum put the phone down, I jumped on her lap and asked her who she had been talking to.

The **trouble with jumping on someone's lap** is you shouldn't really do it if they are holding a cup of tea. Luckily my mum had been talking on the phone for ages, so her tea wasn't very hot. It was still a bit wet though.

When she had dried herself, she told me that the person who had rung her before seven o'clock in the morning was Grampy! Apparently Grampy had walked to the shopping parade early that morning to collect his newspapers, and guess what? When he got to the parade, there were police cars all over the place!

Not outside the newsagent's – outside the fish-and-chip shop!

That's the **trouble with fish and chips**. Burglars can't resist them!

And that's not all they can't resist!!!!!! Not only had the burglars burgled the fish-and-chip shop, they had burgled two actual houses in the same actual night too! And in the same actual town. The same actual town where me, Mum and Nanny and Grampy actually live!

As soon as I found out that two actual houses had been burgled in our actual town, I ran to the window to see if anyone had been burgled in our street too!

But there weren't any police cars to be seen. So I ran back to my mum to hear more.

Mum said that after Grampy had paid for his newspapers, he had bumped into the fish-and-chip-shop owner outside the shop. According to the fish-and-chip-shop owner, burglars had broken into his fish-and-chip shop in the middle of the night. But not only that. According to Grampy they had done it "under the cover of darkness".

The **trouble with the cover of darkness** is it covers you really darkly.

I reckon as soon as a burglar gets right under a cover of darkness, it's a bit like wearing an invisible cloak. Especially if they're wearing a black jumper too. And black trousers. And black shoes and a black mask. Black everything really.

That's what I'd wear if I was a burglar.

Grampy said he reckoned the burglars had probably broken into the fish-and-chip shop

because they were trying to steal all the money in the till. Fish-and-chip shops make loads of money selling fish and chips. Especially large cods and medium skates.

What the burglars didn't know, though, is that the fish-and-chip-shop owner had emptied his till the evening before. So when the burglars tried to steal all the money, they found there wasn't any money in the till to steal!

Mum reckoned that's why they stole some big bags of frozen cods and haddocks instead.

I reckon they might have just

worked up an appetite. Especially if they had burgled two actual houses already.

When I asked what the burglars had stolen from the houses, she said Grampy didn't know. One of the houses that had been burgled was in Holly Way, though, and the other one was in Cypress Drive, which were both almost nearly quite close to where we live!

But Mum didn't know what had been taken. Probably jewels and whopping big tellies.

(Plus salt and vinegar for the burglars' fish and chips.)

CHAPTER 4

As soon as I found out that actual burglars had been doing actual burgling in the actual town where I lived, I knew exactly what I had to do. Number one: Ring Gabby. Number two: Start a detective agency FAST!!! Well, fastish.

The **trouble with starting a detective agency fast** is it gets a whole lot slower when your mum suddenly thinks of loads of other things you need to do first.

Like get dressed, have your breakfast and clean your teeth.

Mum said my detective work would be a whole lot better if I was investigating on a full stomach and without sticky-uppy hair.

When I told her that the burglars' trail would be getting cold and that I really needed to get on the case straight away, she wasn't the slightest bit interested. In fact, she even made me put my breakfast spoon and bowl in the dishwasher! And damp my hair down with a really wet flannel. I mean, what is the matter with her? Hasn't she seen actual detective programmes on the actual telly? Doesn't she know that actual detectives on the actual telly never have time to damp their hair down? Or pick their clothes and toys up off their bedroom floor?

Top detectives just get a phone call, find out there's a burglar and get on the case. FAST!

But not in our house.

Thanks to my mum. In our house, burglars get given loads of time to escape before I'm even allowed to think about starting a detective agency.

I mean, do you know what time it was when I was actually allowed to ring Gabby? Do you know what time it was when I was actually allowed to tell her that she needed to get over to my house really fast because we were soon going to be on the trail of dangerous criminals?

Twenty past eight!

Oh well, better late than never, I suppose . . .

CHAPTER 5

When I told Gabby that a house in Holly Way and another in Cypress Drive had been burgled, PLUS the fish-and-chip shop had been burgled too, she squeaked like a guinea pig! Gabby said this was easily the best start to a summer holiday we had ever had. And she was right!

When I told her we were going to catch the burglars ourselves by starting our very own detective agency, she nearly dropped the phone!

That's the **trouble with starting a detective agency**. It's exciting and dangerous at the same time.

I said it wouldn't matter how dangerous things got as long as we practised our martial arts skills in my bedroom first. Burglars are defenceless against karate chops and really good wrestling holds. Especially if you get them round the neck.

Gabby said her mum kept a pair of pink furry handcuffs in her bedroom and she would ask if we could borrow them. Then we made a list of all the other detective equipment we were going to need.

The **trouble with magnifying glasses** is no one in Gabby's family has got one and neither has my mum.

Plus no one had any bulletproof jackets we could borrow either. So we decided we wouldn't put them on our list at all.

Luckily we had all the other things we needed:

Notebooks (for doing interviews)
Pens (for taking statements)

My mum's camera (for
    photographing evidence)
Orange squash (for drinking after
    chasing burglars)
Crisps (for energy)
Icing sugar (for fingerprinting)

All we had to do next was meet up,
decide on a name for our detective
agency, do our combat training and
get started!

CHAPTER 6

By ten past nine, Gabby and I were both black belts in Burglar Fu (which is a bit like Kung Fu, only it's better for fighting baddies who are trying to bonk you on the head with silver candlesticks or flat-screen tellies).

By quarter past nine, the D & G Burglar Bashing and Catching Agency was nearly open for business!

When I told Mum that Gabby and I were starting our own detective agency and that she wasn't going to be in it, she didn't seem bothered at all.

Gabby said behaviour like that was very suspicious – if my mum carried on not wanting to chase burglars, people might think she was on the burglars' side. I said there was no way that a burglar would want my mum in her gang. For a start, she's usually in bed by ten o'clock, she'd never be able to carry a fifty-inch-screen telly by herself, she never drives above about forty-five miles an hour, plus she never wears black.

We still made her the first name on our list of suspects though.

Because we wanted to try out our pens.

After we'd made sure our notebooks and pens were working, we went through our list again and packed our crime detection bags.

The **trouble with crime detection bags** is they don't want to be too big and they don't want to be too small.

If your crime detection bag is too big, it might slow you down when you're chasing a burglar. But if it's too small, you might not be able to fill it with valuable evidence, such as burglar masks that have been thrown into bushes in a hurry, or burglar trainers that have come off in deep mud.

The best crime detection bags have two right-sized compartments: one that's just the right size for valuable evidence and one that's just the right size for all the really important crime detection things you need.

Especially icing sugar.

The **trouble with icing sugar** is mums don't like you borrowing it.

Especially if you need the whole box.

Icing sugar is the most important thing to have in your crime detection bag if you need to dust for fingerprints. Trouble is, mums just want to use it for icing cakes.

When Gabby asked to borrow the whole box of icing sugar out of her kitchen cupboard, her mum stopped her before she could even put it in her bag. Even when Gabby explained what we needed it for, her mum wouldn't let her have any. Not even a spoonful.

Or any handcuffs.

So we decided to borrow the icing sugar from my kitchen cupboard instead. Without asking my mum. That way she couldn't say no.

The **trouble with borrowing things without asking** is it helps if the person you're not asking isn't there when you decide to not ask them.

Trouble is, my mum was. She was standing in the kitchen, right in the way of the cupboard, so there was no way we could take the box out of the cupboard without her noticing.

So we needed to create a diversion.

The **trouble with diversions** is they have to be really good or your mum won't look the other way for long enough.

If your mum doesn't look away for long enough, it doesn't give you enough time to get the box of icing sugar out of the cupboard and put it in your bag without her noticing.

The **trouble with a pretend-coughing-fit diversion** is you need lots of room to do it in. Which was OK actually, because the kitchen door was open and it was a lovely sunny day outside.

It was Gabby who did the pretend coughs. Actually, they started off as coughs, but then they became more like chokes.

At first my mum just stayed by the cupboard and patted her on the back, but when I gave Gabby the secret wink, she did her

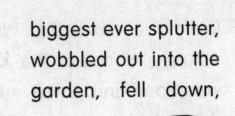

biggest ever splutter, wobbled out into the garden, fell down,

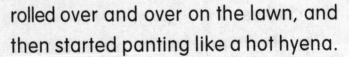

rolled over and over on the lawn, and then started panting like a hot hyena. Which meant my mum had no choice but to run out into the garden to save her.

Gabby did a really, really good job at pretend coughing, because not only did I have time to put the whole box of icing sugar in my bag, I had time to get the camera from the drawer in the lounge, plus put some bonus scissors in my bag too! (Just in case we got tied up by burglars during our investigations and needed to cut through the ropes.)

I think my mum was quite surprised when Gabby recovered from her coughing fit so quickly. She was quite puffed out too, after carrying her back into the kitchen.

She made Gabby have a drink

of water and do about twelve really deep breaths before she would let her start playing with me again. But at 9.29 she gave Gabby the all clear.

By 9.30 the D & G Burglar Bashing and Catching Company was finally in business!

And things were going really well until about 9.31.

CHAPTER 7

I could NOT believe it when, just as Gabby and I stepped out of the front door to start our investigation, my mum shouted, "HAVE FUN, DAISY. AND DON'T GO FURTHER THAN THE END OF THE ROAD!"

Don't go further than the end of the road?!!!!!!!!!

The **trouble with not being allowed to go further than the end of the road** is it makes doing a burglar investigation almost impossible!

I mean, how can anyone do a proper burglar investigation if they're not allowed to go further than the end of the road?

Scooby Doo is allowed to go further than the end of his road. Plus that detective on the telly with the funny moustache is always, always, always going further than the end of his road. Even Gabby is allowed to go further than the end of her road!

So why not ME?

Mum said I had never been allowed to play further than the end of the road without her being with me, and if Gabby and me wanted to chase burglars, we would have to do it where she could see us. Because that way she would know we were safe.

SAFE?

Since when was chasing burglars meant to be safe!?

When I told my mum that Gabby's mum lets Gabby go loads further than the end of the road she lives in, and I should be allowed to as well, it didn't make any difference at all.

Mum said I knew the rules – if I didn't like them, we could play in my bedroom instead.

PLAY!!!!!???

We weren't meant to be *playing* at

catching burglars! We were meant to be catching them FOR REAL!

I'm telling you, I have never slammed my front door so hard.

When Gabby and me got outside on the pavement, we weren't quite sure how our investigation should begin. We had planned to walk to Holly Way and Cypress Drive to dust for fingerprints, look for tracks, search for clues, interview the people who had been burgled, write down all the things that had been stolen,

take photographs of their safes, see if their guard dogs had been given poisonous sausages, plus ask their neighbours if they'd seen or heard anything suspicious in the night, under the cover of darkness.

Trouble is, Holly Way and Cypress Drive were both further than the end of my road. So we couldn't.

Then Gabby had a brilliant idea. She said that after the burglars had done all their burgling, they might have come down my street in their getaway car! If they'd come down my street in their getaway car, then they might have left some getaway clues!

The **trouble with getaway clues** is you need really good eyesight to see them.

Especially if you haven't got a magnifying glass in your crime detection bag.

The first clue we picked up was a piece of chewed-up chewing gum.

clue 1

Gabby reckoned one of the burglars had probably been chewing it on the way home in the getaway car, but all the taste had run out. So he'd thrown it out of the window.

The second clue we found was a little piece of metal. I reckoned it might have been a snipping from some wire cutters, but Gabby was sure it had come off a bullet.

clue 2

Next we found a piece of dirty paper that was definitely the corner of a ransom note.

clue 3

Plus a piece of string that looked like it had come from a tying-up rope.

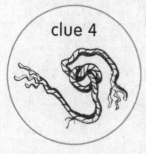

clue 4

Every time we found a getaway clue, we took a photo of it and then put it into our bag.

By the kerb outside number 56 we found a half-sucked burglar's Polo mint. (Don't worry. I didn't eat it!)

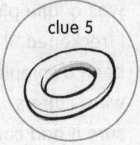

clue 5

Outside the gate of number 78 we found some suspicious leaves.

clue 6

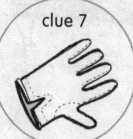
clue 7

On the wall outside number 84 we found a burglar's glove.

And underneath an empty snail shell beneath a bush beside a wall beside the gate to number 106, we even found some dandruff that a burglar had scratched from his head!

clue 8

After about an hour of looking, we had around twenty getaway clues in our bag.

But it was at the top of my road that we found our biggest and best one!

The **trouble with skid marks** is you can't put them in your bag. Because they're stuck to the road.

The **trouble with roads** is they are really dangerous places to stand in the middle of.

Which meant taking photographs of the skid mark could be a bit tricky.

At first we thought we would only be able to take pictures from the kerb, but we were wrong. Because guess who came along on his bike, at just the right time?

Dylan!

Dylan is a really cool boy who lives in my road. He's ten, which means he's allowed to cycle much further than the end of our road without being told off.

When we told Dylan what we were doing, he said he was on the trail of the burglars too. He said everyone in the whole town was talking about the burglaries, and he had already cycled over to Holly Way and Cypress Drive to see what he could see.

Apparently the house in Holly Way had broken glass in its front door and the house in Cypress Drive had a police car outside it!

Dylan said that the policeman sitting in the car wouldn't tell him what had been stolen, but from the look on his face it was jewellery at least, possibly even gold bars.

After Dylan had used our camera to take close-up photos of the getaway skid mark, he used his special detective vision to tell us how fast the burglars had been going, how many burglars there were in the car, what car they were driving, and the first four letters of their number plate.

Gabby and I didn't know you could tell so much from the shape of a skid mark, but Dylan said that when you've been cycling as long as he has, reading skid marks becomes a real skill.

Dylan said if we let him join our crime detection agency, he could get us loads more clues from Holly Way and Cypress Drive, plus the fish-and-chip shop as well. Double plus, he would get his magnifying glass from his bedroom and let us use it in our investigations too!

Gabby and me knew that the burglars would have no chance of getting away if we had a magnifying glass, so it was decided there and then.

The D & G Burglar Bashing and Catching Agency now had an extra D!

CHAPTER 8

The **trouble with magnifying glasses** is they should really have three handles. Then three people could hold them at the same time.

Seeing burglar clues a zillion times bigger is the business!

Dylan said that the little bit of metal that Gabby had found was definitely from a bullet.

It might even have been from a bullet fired by a machine gun! But he wouldn't be able to tell without doing further investigations.

The **trouble** **with** **further** **investigations** is you can't just do them in the street.

So we decided we would all go back to my house to further investigate there.

When we got back, we set up a further investigation laboratory in my bedroom. Dylan said that the tiny bit of bullet metal had been fired from a Russian machine gun that had the capability to launch missiles as well. Then he said we must spread all our clues out on my bedside table, and go through them one by one to check for DNA.

The **trouble with DNA** is Gabby and I didn't know what DNA was. Until Dylan told us. According to Dylan, DNA is the most microscopicest bit of a person you can get.

It's smaller than the speckiest speck and it has the person's name written all over it.

Dylan says that you can find DNA in spit, dribble, a cough, a bit of hair, a bit of sneeze, a bit of fingernail, even a drip of sweat. All you have to do is put your clue with the DNA in it under a really powerful microscope and you can see precisely which burglar it belongs to.

The **trouble with powerful microscopes** is we only had one magnifying glass to look through.

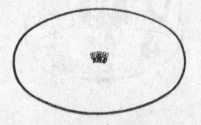

Luckily Dylan was born with magnifying eyes.

According to Dylan's magnifying eyes, our clues were swarming with DNA!

He said there was burglar dribble in the chewing gum, fingerprint juice on the ransom note, fingernail specks inside the glove, tooth marks on the Polo, hairstyle patterns in the dandruff, and struggle-sweat all over the string.

After about half an hour, Dylan finished his further investigations and told us to have our notebooks at the ready.

This is the important information he asked us to write down:

1. There are definitely three burglars.
2. All of them are Russian.
3. Their names are Olaf, Igor and Boris.
4. Olaf has brown hair.
5. The other two have black hair.
6. Boris has a limp.
7. Igor has a moustache.
8. Olaf is the one with the machine gun.
9. The person who has been tied up is a Russian hairdresser called Saskia.
10. The car they are driving is a red Ferrari.
11. Olaf likes Polos.
12. Igor prefers chewing gum.
13. My house is going to be burgled next.

The **trouble with finding out that your house is going to be burgled next** is you have to tell your mum straight away.

Trouble is, she was in the garden talking to our neighbour Mrs Pike. My mum is always talking to Mrs Pike. Even when I tugged her elbow, she didn't stop talking, talking, talking and talking. So we didn't have any choice really. We had to burglar-proof my house without asking.

CHAPTER 9

The **trouble with making your house burglar-proof** is you need SmartWater.

The **trouble with SmartWater** is Gabby and me hadn't heard of it either.

Dylan told us that SmartWater was the very latest thing in catching burglars, and that he'd seen it used by the police in loads of crime detection programmes.

Apparently, SmartWater is water that's very clever. Because not only does it make burglars very wet when it squirts on them, it covers them with stuff that won't wash off.

Even if you use a flannel it won't come off.

Even if you use soap!

The **trouble with stuff that won't wash off** is, if you're a squirted burglar, the police will always catch

you in the end. Because as soon as the police arrest you and point an ultra-violent light at you, all the SmartWater squirts show up on your clothes and your skin.

Which means you definitely did it.

So you're definitely going to go to prison.

When I told Dylan that I didn't think my mum had any SmartWater in her cupboard, he said it wouldn't matter because we could make our own; as long as we could find a bucket we could fill with water and some ingredients that wouldn't come off.

When I went back into the garden to ask if we could borrow the red bucket, my mum was still talking to Mrs Pike. And talking and talking and talking. Even when I tugged her T-shirt, she kept on talking.

Which meant I had no choice really. I had to borrow our red bucket without asking too. And some ingredients that wouldn't come off. Like:

The ink from Mum's pen

 cake colourings

Tabasco sauce

tomato sauce

brown sauce

 shoe polish

mustard powder

 a little bit of milk

and a fish finger

Once we'd finished stirring our bucket, Dylan reckoned we hadn't just made SmartWater, we had probably made the smartest water ever invented. He said that once we had caught the burglars with it, we could probably sell our recipe to the police for loads of money and retire from school and everything.

Trouble is, it wasn't burglars that we caught. It was my mum.

CHAPTER 10

It was Dylan's idea to set burglar traps all over my house, not mine. And it was Gabby's idea to put them in my front garden too. Dylan and Gabby said that burglar-proofing my house would be brilliant fun and they were right. Trouble is, I'm not sure my mum quite agreed. When she finally came in from the garden after talking and talking and talking to Mrs Pike, she wasn't expecting to find a bucket of SmartWater balanced on top of the kitchen door.

Or trip wires in the kitchen.

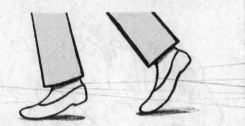

Or marbles and pickled onions on the carpet in the hallway.

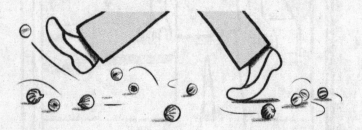

Or custard and rice pudding in the flowerbeds in the front garden.

Or olive oil on the window ledges of the lounge.

When I told her that we were going to be burgled next, and we'd made our house and front garden burglar-proof, she wasn't the slightest bit grateful.

Even when I explained how SmartWater worked, and that the trip wires would double-stop any burglars from getting across our kitchen floor, and that even if they did get across our kitchen floor, they would fall over on the marbles and pickled onions in the hallway, or if they tried to climb in through a front window, the olive oil on the window ledges would make it far too slippery for them to get a grip, even in gloves, and that burglar footprints were impossible to get really good photos of when it's hot because the ground is too hard and their feet don't stick in properly – even if a burglar just came up to the front of our house and looked through the window, they'd leave really good footprints in the rice pudding or custard we'd put in the flowerbeds, because custard and rice pudding are much softer than hard ground.

I tried explaining everything!

But I think Mum was too wet to listen.

The **trouble with being too wet to listen** is it makes you really unreasonable. Especially if it's the second time you've been made wet in one day.

Mum didn't thank us for burglar-proofing the house or anything! In fact, do you know what she did? She told Gabby and Dylan that it was time for them to go home!

Can you believe that? After all the detective work and burglar-proofing we had done?!

Gabby and Dylan said they were actually thinking about going home for lunch about that time anyway, and they would leave their crime detection equipment in my bedroom for now.

Which meant that the D, G & D Burglar Bashing and Catching Agency was now down to just one person – me!

And all thanks to my mum.

Oh well, at least I had the magnifying glass all to myself.

CHAPTER 11

When my mum got out of the shower, she still seemed a bit cross. She must have used a really good shower gel to wash our SmartWater off with, because I couldn't see any stains on her face or arms or anything. Mind you, I didn't get a look at her under ultra-violent light.

After she had calmed down a bit more, we had a sandwich for lunch, then she asked me to lock the kitchen door and close all the windows in the house, because we were going out.

As it was the first day of the summer holidays, I half thought she might have been taking me to the zoo, or a safari park or the seaside. Instead, it turned out we were going to the post office.

The **trouble with post offices** is they are nowhere near as exciting as zoos and seasides.

UNLESS . . .

Wait for it . . .

Unless the post office you are

going to just happens to be inside a certain newspaper shop! A certain newspaper shop that just happens to be right next door to a certain fish-and-chip shop! The same certain fish-and-chip shop that just happens to have been burgled in our actual town the actual night before!!!

As soon as I realized we would be going right up close to the actual fish-and-chip shop that had been burgled in our town, I grabbed my crime detection bag! This was my big chance not only to see an actual place that had been actually burgled by actual burglars, but also to do some actual fingerprinting too!

In the car on the way to the post office, things got even more exciting, because Mum told me what she and Mrs Pike had been talking and talking and talking about.

Apparently, at six o'clock that evening, there was going to be an emergency Crimestoppers meeting at the village hall. And everyone in the whole town was invited, including me!

Which meant if I got some really good clues from the fish-and-chip shop, I might be able to tell Dylan, Gabby and the whole town where the burglars were hiding! We might even get a reward!

Tax disc!

When I asked my mum how many stamps she was going to be buying at the post office, she said she wasn't going to be buying stamps at all. She was going to be buying something called car tax.

Apparently car tax is the round

piece of coloured paper that you see stuck to the front of car windows. If you look carefully at the coloured circle, you can see it has a date printed on it. When you get past that date, you have to buy another car tax straight away, or you're not allowed to drive your car. You're not even allowed to park it on the road.

The **trouble with buying another car tax** is it costs a lot of money.

Mum said that her car tax had run out three weeks ago, but it had taken her all this time to save up enough to afford a new one. Plus she'd been really busy.

I said that if I got a reward for catching the burglars, I would give her all the money she needed to buy as many car taxes as she wanted.

Then I started thinking.

If my mum was driving her car but the date on her car tax said she shouldn't have been driving her car, plus when she wasn't driving it, she was parking it on the road – but if you don't have car tax, you're not meant to park your car on the road – did that mean what I thought it meant? Did that actually mean that my mum was a criminal too?

When I asked my mum if she was a criminal, she told me not to be so silly. She said she had to park her car somewhere, and in any case she had hardly driven her car at all since her car tax had run out. Plus, when she had driven her car, she had only done really short journeys. Like to the shops or to visit Nanny and Grampy.

When I said that she had driven her car to aerobics and aerobics was right on the other side of town, she started to get a bit cross with me.

Which was a bit unfair really, because *I* wasn't the one who had been driving everywhere without car tax, *she* was.

Then, when I remembered she had driven to Ikea last Sunday, and Ikea was even further away than aerobics, she stopped the car altogether and asked me if I'd like to walk to the post office instead.

The **trouble with walking to the post office** is top detectives don't walk anywhere.

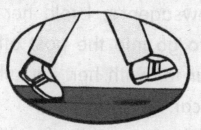

They always drive or get driven. Because they're too important.

And anyway, there wasn't much point, because guess where we were really close to now . . .

Yes, the fish-and-chip shop!

At last it was time for me to do my first fingerprinting.

CHAPTER 12

When Mum parked the car outside the newsagent's, I told her I didn't want to go into the post office and buy car tax with her. I'd rather wait in the car.

Which was a bit of a fib really, because as soon as my mum walked into the post office, I undid my seatbelt, made sure I had everything I needed in my crime detection bag, put the strap over my shoulder, jumped out of the car and got ready to go to work.

When I saw the broken window in the fish-and-chip-shop door, I nearly wet myself. A burglar had actually smashed the glass to get inside! I couldn't see the actual broken bits of glass because they had been covered up with brown sticky tape. Broken glass can be one of the most dangerous things in the world unless it's covered up.

When I saw that the fish-and-chip shop was still open, I was even more surprised! I mean, how could a fish-and-chip shop still be open if all of its cods and haddocks had been stolen? Then I remembered that fish-and-chip shops do chicken pies as well. And sausages in batter. So they probably had other things left in their cupboard that they could still sell.

The **trouble with a fish-and-chip shop being open** is it makes the door really hard to do fingerprinting experiments on.

Because every time you try and sprinkle your icing sugar over the sticky tape, people keep coming in and out.

Plus they give you really funny looks when they see what you are doing.

So after about three tries, I decided to do the big window at the front of the shop instead.

The **trouble with big windows at the front of shops** is they can use all your icing sugar up really quickly if you're not careful.

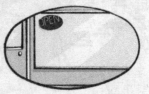

At first I tried to shake as much icing sugar as I could over the actual window, but it wouldn't stick to the glass. So I decided to do the window ledge instead.

Sprinkling icing sugar on window ledges is much better than doing it on windows, because you can get a much deeper lot on. But my icing sugar totally ran out before I was quite at the very end of the window ledge.

That's when I realized I didn't have a fingerprint brush.

The **trouble with not having a fingerprint brush** is it means you have to use your fingers to brush the fingerprint powder on instead.

The **trouble with brushing fingerprint powder on with your fingers** is it means you get your own fingerprints all over the burglars' fingerprints that you're meant to be dusting.

Luckily I had Dylan's magnifying glass to help me tell which ones were which.

I reckon I'd found about seventeen really good burglar fingerprints before I realized how many people were looking at me through the window of the fish-and-chip shop.

They weren't just looking either. They were staring and pointing.

The **trouble with people staring and pointing at you** is it puts you off when you're taking your photographs. Especially if one of the people is the owner of the shop.

I didn't know he was the owner of the shop until he actually came out of the shop and started getting cross with me.

"Why are you taking photos of my window?!" he shouted. "Is that icing sugar!? It better not be icing sugar!"

I was going to tell him that I was on the trail of the burglars, which meant I was actually doing him a favour, but before I could even begin to explain, someone else started shouting at me too.

It was my mum.

The **trouble with two people shouting at you at the same time** is you don't know which way to look first. Or which way to run.

When I saw my mum, I thought at first that she was having a hissy fit about her icing sugar. But then I saw the two police people she was pointing at.

"Get in the car, Daisy! Get in the car now!" she shouted as I raced back to the car.

"DON'T FORGET TO DO UP YOUR SEATBELT! DON'T FORGET TO DO UP YOUR SEATBELT!"

she shouted as I climbed back into my seat.

"Don't ask questions! Don't ask questions!" she shouted as we screeched away in our car.

The **trouble with someone saying everything twice** is it makes you wonder who is panicking the most.

That's when I realized that it wasn't me who had been escaping from the policemen. It was my mum! That's when I realized we were about to do a getaway of our own!

CHAPTER 13

When I asked my mum why we were doing a getaway in our car, she said it was because she didn't want the policemen to see that our car tax had run out. Which was a bit odd really, because I thought that that was why she had gone to the post office in the first place – to get some new car tax for our car!

That's when Mum told me about the queue.

The **trouble with queues in the post office** is they can be really long.

And slow.

Mum said the queue she was in was SO long and SO slow she wasn't even close to getting our new car tax when the police car pulled up outside.

Which is why she panicked.

Because if the policemen got out of their car . . .

And walked past our car . . .

And saw the round coloured tax paper on our windscreen . . .

And noticed that the date had run out . . .

Mum would get into trouble!

BIG TROUBLE!

So she panicked.

She panicked at precisely the same time that I was panicking. Which probably made us both look VERY suspicious INDEED!

Luckily we did a really good getaway! Which was actually really, really exciting.

When I looked through the back window of our car, I hoped I might see a police car chasing us with a blue light flashing and everything. Which would have been even more exciting.

But there was no one chasing us at all.

Mum said the two policemen had hopefully come to talk to the fish-and-chip-shop owner about the burglary and probably hadn't even noticed us.

Which was good because I didn't want to get told off.

But then my mum noticed her icing-sugar box.

The **trouble with mums noticing icing-sugar boxes** is when they see them, they want to know what you're doing with them.

When I told her I'd been using her icing sugar to dust for fingerprints, she nearly crashed the car. Then, when I told her that there wasn't any icing sugar left in the box, she went the colour of tomato sauce. Because it was a new box.

The **trouble with your mum going the colour of tomato sauce** is you don't think there are any worse colours your mum's face can go.

But then she went purple. Because she suddenly realized that not only had I used up all her icing sugar, I had taken it without asking in the first place, plus I hadn't stayed in the car like I'd promised. Which meant I'd stolen something as well as told fibs, on top of using up all her icing sugar.

On top of covering her with SmartWater.

On top of setting burglar traps all over the house with Dylan and Gabby.

We didn't say much more in the car after that.

CHAPTER 14

When we got home, I decided to go to my room.

Mum said it was her idea that I went upstairs to my bedroom, but it definitely wasn't. Because I'd actually already decided to go to my bedroom about two seconds before she decided that I should go to my bedroom. Which made it my decision.

Deciding to spend the afternoon on my own in my bedroom was really handy actually, because I didn't have to see Mum's face turning any other

funny colours, plus I had loads of
fingerprint photos that I needed to
investigate.

The **trouble with fingerprint photos** is they don't come out very well on my mum's camera. Because it's not a proper police camera.

Even the pictures I had taken through Dylan's magnifying glass still looked very blurry and mostly only like icing sugar. That's what happens when you don't have a proper police camera to take your photos.

Luckily I suddenly developed super magnifying detective vision just like Dylan, so not only was I able to see and draw really good pictures of all the fingerprints I had photographed, I also worked out loads of new facts about each burglar; things even Dylan couldn't see!

These are my fingerprint findings:

Fingerprints belonging to Olaf

1st finger, right hand shows definite signs of pointing a lot. Probably at policemen.

Thumb

1st and 2nd fingers.

Right hand: definitely used for picking locks.

Thumb, left hand

used for giving the all clear.

Fingerprints belonging to Igor

Thumb and 1st finger, right hand: definitely used for safe-cracking and tying people up (like Saskia).

1st finger, left hand: probably picks his nose.

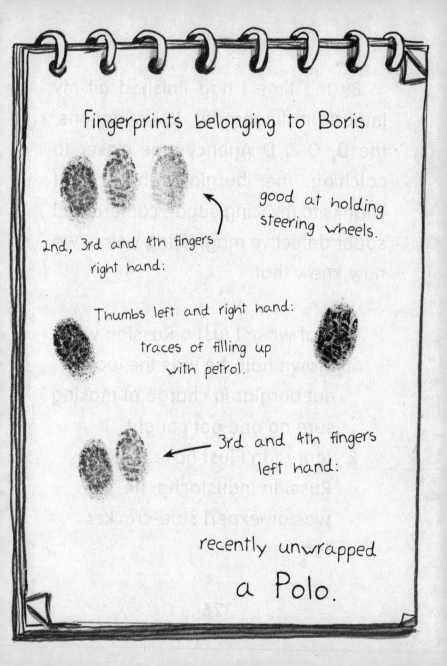

By the time I had finished all my important fingerprint investigations, the D, G & D Agency was closer to catching the burglars than ever! Thanks to my icing sugar, camera and super detective magnifying vision, we now knew that:

1. Olaf wasn't just a Russian with brown hair; he was the look-out burglar in charge of making sure no one got caught.
2. Igor didn't just have a black Russian moustache; he was an expert safe-cracker too.

3. Boris wasn't just better at
   shaving than Igor, he ate Polos
   without crunching them and
   always drove the getaway car
   (probably because of his limp).

All I had to do now was meet up
with Dylan and Gabby again and tell
them what I'd discovered!
Plus:

1. Eat the crisps I'd put in my
   crime detection bag.
2. Drink my orange squash.
3. Get ready for the
   Crimestoppers meeting.

Oh yes, and:

4. Be allowed out of my room.

CHAPTER 15

I was finally allowed out of my room at about quarter past five. But only because I needed to eat my dinner.

When Mrs Pike knocked on our front door at 5.45, I was standing downstairs in the hallway with my crime detection bag all packed and itching to go!

But I still refused to let her in. Because she might have been a burglar in disguise.

When Mrs Pike looked at me through the letterbox and said she wasn't a burglar in disguise, I said that's exactly what a burglar in disguise would say if they were a burglar in disguise pretending not to be a burglar in disguise.

Then Mum told me not to be so silly and made me open the door, so I had to let her in. (But I still wrote down a description of her in my notebook.)

Mum said there was no way she could drive our car to a Crimestoppers meeting. Especially as it didn't have any car tax and double especially as the car park was going to be full of police cars.

When I found out that Mrs Pike would be driving us instead, I was actually quite pleased, because Mrs Pike's car has electric windows, plus it can go up to 120 miles an hour. Plus I didn't want to be arrested.

When we got to the village hall, there were absolutely loads of people queuing to get in. Mum said the queue was about ten times longer than the one in the post office! Which was quite handy actually because it gave me a chance to talk to Dylan and Gabby before the meeting began.

Dylan and Gabby were really

impressed with my fingerprint investigations. Dylan said he'd cycled back over to Holly Way after lunch, and was now certain that the burglars were armed with machine guns. Plus they had a bow and arrow that fired arrowheads dipped in sleeping gas.

When I asked him how he could tell, Gabby showed me a feather she had found in Cypress Drive.

At first I thought it was just a pigeon's feather. But Dylan said it was much more than that. He said the burglars were using pigeon feathers just like the one Gabby had found to make the feathery bits for the tops of their arrows.

He said once they had made the feathery bits for their arrows, they would dip the pointy bits in sleeping gas, point them up at the sky and

shoot them down the chimney of the house they were going to burgle.

Once the arrow stuck in the carpet, the sleeping gas would start to work.

The **trouble with sleeping gas** is it means the burglars can break into your house even if you haven't gone to bed. Because as soon as you sniff the sleeping gas you'll be asleep in about two seconds anyway. Which means you won't see or hear a thing!

Dylan said we easily had enough evidence to catch the burglars now. It was so exciting!

When we got through the doors, I found that loads of my school friends had come to the meeting with their parents too! And everyone was just as excited about the burglars as we were.

Nishta Bagwhat said her mum and dad were buying an actual burglar alarm for their house!

David Alexander said his dad had put brand-new window locks on all the downstairs windows in his house.

Paula Potts said she had hidden her favourite dolly under her pillow.

Barry Morely said he had hidden his *Star Wars* Lego under his bed.

And Colin Kettle said he had taken all the money out of his piggy bank that morning and hidden it inside his socks! (Which is why he was limping, I think.)

When I told everyone that me, Gabby and Dylan had been on the trail of the burglars all day, and that we were really close to catching them, everyone was really interested to find out more.

Except Jack Beechwhistle.

The **trouble with Jack Beechwhistle** is he thinks he knows how to catch burglars too. Except he doesn't.

Jack Beechwhistle said that if burglars tried to break into his house, they would find themselves in dead trouble. Because his dad kept a baseball bat by his bed.

Which is rubbish. Because Russians don't even play baseball.

Then Jack Beechwhistle said his dad was going to buy a wolverine for a guard dog too.

Dylan said there was no way anyone could buy a wolverine for a guard dog because pet shops don't sell them, plus wolverines are the most dangerous dogs in the world.

And Dylan should know, because he's ten.

So Jack Beechwhistle changed it to a hyena instead.

Which is rubbish as well, because hyenas live in Africa. Plus their teeth are far too wild and gnashy to be a pet.

When I asked Jack if he'd done any burglar investigations, he said he had but he wasn't going to tell us what he'd found out in case there was a reward. If there was going to be a reward, he wanted to keep it all to himself.

He wouldn't even tell us how many burglars he thought there were.

Or what the getaway driver's favourite sweet was.

I said that if he wasn't going to tell us any of his clues, we weren't going to tell him any of ours.

But he said he didn't care.

So I said we didn't care either.

Which made him stick his tongue out.

Which made me stick my tongue out.

Which made him try and look inside my crime detection bag.

Which made me push him away.

Which made him push me back.

Which made me call him a "poopy face".

Which made him call me "gorilla features".

Which made me want to arrest him.

And send him to prison for about ten years.

Without any pillows.

Or breakfast.

Or loo roll.

Honestly, Jack Beechwhistle can be so childish sometimes.

CHAPTER 16

When we got inside the hall, we sat as far away from Jack Beechwhistle as we could. Mrs Pike sat next to Mum, Mum sat next to me, I sat next to Gabby, Gabby sat next to her mum and dad, Gabby's dad sat next to Dylan, and Dylan sat next to his mum and dad. Then we changed over, because I decided it would be better if the D, G & D Agency all sat together, so Gabby's mum switched with Dylan, which meant me, Gabby and Dylan were now all in a line.

Plus it meant that D, G & D were all sitting in the right order.

At first I couldn't see very much at the Crimestoppers meeting because Barry Morely's dad suddenly came along and sat down right in front of me.

The **trouble with Barry Morely's dad** is he's really tall. But it was OK, because after I tapped him on the head with Dylan's magnifying glass, he bobbed down really low.

When his head was out of the way, I could see absolutely everything. I could see the stage, I could see a big white screen, and I could see a lady in a green dress talking into a microphone.

The **trouble with microphones** is you really need to switch them on before you start talking. Otherwise the people at the back of the hall can't hear what you are saying.

At first I don't think the lady realized her microphone wasn't switched on because her lips were moving for ages before someone at the front of the hall finally got up onto the stage and turned it on for her.

Which meant the only words we actually heard her say were "Ian Pennick".

After that, all I could hear was clapping.

The **trouble with clapping** is it makes you start clapping too. Even if you don't know why you're clapping.

Luckily a policeman walked onto the stage at the same time as we were clapping, and when he took the microphone from the lady, we worked out who he was.

"Good evening, ladies and

gentlemen," he said. "My name is Sergeant Ian Pennick. Thank you so much for attending this Crimestoppers meeting at such short notice."

As soon as he said the word "Crimestoppers", I took my crime detection notebook out of my bag and winked at Gabby and Dylan.

"What clues shall we tell him about first?" I whispered.

"Tell him the burglars are Russian," whispered Dylan.

The **trouble with telling a police sergeant that burglars are Russian** is you have to wait for him to stop talking first.

The **trouble with waiting for a police sergeant to stop talking** is he doesn't flipping stop talking at all! Especially at a Crimestoppers meeting.

First of all, he told everyone how long he'd been in the police force. Then he told us how much he knew about our town. Then he put loads of numbers and charts up on the big white screen. Then he started talking about burglaries that hadn't even happened in our town; they'd happened all over the country instead. Then he told us that the chances of us being burgled too were

Boring!

really small because the burglars
had almost definitely moved on to
another town and were probably
doing burglaries
there instead. Then
he told us to padlock
our sheds just in
case.

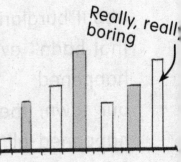

Really
boring

Really, really
boring

Then he showed us
some more charts,
and then some

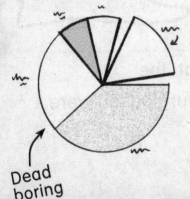

more numbers, and
then some pictures of
cakes with different

Dead
boring

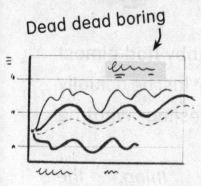

Dead dead boring

coloured slices, and then he talked about some squiggles that looked like a spider with wonky legs.

Honestly, if we'd had to buy tickets to listen to him, I'd definitely have asked for my money back.

Me, Dylan and Gabby had almost fallen asleep, when at last he actually said something interesting. What he said was this:

"The important thing, the important thing for all of us, is that every man, woman and child here today becomes the eyes and ears of the community."

The **trouble with being the eyes and ears of the community** is it's definitely a full-time job.

Because it means if your neighbours are away on holiday, you're meant to watch their houses in case they get burgled. If you see someone acting suspiciously in your street, you're meant to write down their description. Or if you see a car driving suspiciously down your road, you're meant to write down its registration number too! You have to look and listen out for absolutely everything!

Which was perfect! Because not only did me, Gabby and Dylan all have eyes and ears, we had the whole of the summer holidays to use them!

Then things got even more interesting, because once I had written down the local police station's twenty-four-hour Crime-stoppers emergency hotline telephone number (open every day of the week between the hours of two and five in the afternoon except Tuesdays or Thursdays, not including weekends), the police sergeant asked everyone in the audience if we had any questions.

At first I thought everyone would put their hand up. But they didn't! The only one that put their hand up was me!

"Did you know the burglars are Russian?" I asked.

And guess what? He didn't!

So I put my hand up again.

"Did you know the getaway driver likes Polos?" I asked.

And guess what? He didn't!

"Ask him if he knows what the reward is," whispered Gabby.

"Ask him if he's wearing a bulletproof vest," whispered Dylan.

"Ask him if he can tell us how many jewels have been stolen," said Gabby.

"Ask him if he's found any arrows stuck to the carpet, " said Dylan.

So I did.

And guess what? He didn't and he wasn't and he couldn't and he hadn't!!!!

Which was a bit rubbish really, because if I'd been an actual police sergeant doing an actual police investigation using actual police cameras and actual police microscopes and actual police fingerprint powder, including actual police fingerprint brushes, I would have known the answers to everything.

After I'd asked about four more things, Mum said I should stop asking questions and let other people have a go. Which was a bit annoying really, because the **trouble with letting other people have a go** is if they're grown-ups they ask all the wrong things.

Like:

"Will you be putting more policemen on the streets?"

Or:

"Can you recommend the most reliable type of window lock?"

Or:

"Can you explain the numbers on that chart again?"

I mean, how is anyone supposed to catch a burglar asking really, really boring questions like those?

So I put my hand up again.

But my mum tried to make me put it down.

But she couldn't reach me properly.

So I kept it up.

I don't think the police sergeant wanted to hear what my next question was, but because no one else had their hand up, he had no choice. Which was good really, because my next question was a really, really, really good one. In fact, it was so good, everyone looked at me when I asked it!

"Do you think the cods and haddocks have started to thaw yet?" I asked. "Because if the cods and haddocks have started to thaw out, then they will have started to drip. And if they have started to drip, then

there could be a trail
of cod and haddock
drips leading all
the way back to the
burglars' hideout!"

When the police sergeant heard
my cods and haddocks question, I
don't think he knew what to say. Or if
he did know what to say, he certainly
didn't say it. In fact, he didn't say
one word at all. He just puffed his
cheeks out and looked at his watch.

Which was a bit annoying.

So I put my hand up again. But
this time my mum reached over and
grabbed me. Except she didn't grab

me, she grabbed my bag. Which meant I got away. Which gave me a chance to ask my best question of the night. A question so good that . . . guess what . . . EVERYONE clapped me when I said it!!!!!! (Except the police sergeant and the lady in the green dress.)

"Do you actually know how to catch burglars, because it doesn't sound like you do?" I said.

There were no more questions at the Crimestoppers meeting after that.

CHAPTER 17

When we got outside, everyone told me how good my questions had been. Even grown-ups! Even Jack Beechwhistle!!

On the way home, I started practising being the eyes and ears of the community. Mrs Pike told my mum that the family who lived across the road from us had actually gone on holiday to Portugal, so I was definitely going to have my eyes and ears on their house when I got home.

Being the eyes and ears of the community and sitting in Mrs Pike's car at the same time was actually quite difficult, because Mrs Pike drives much faster than Mum.

The **trouble with fast driving** is it means you need fast eyes and ears.

Eyes mostly, because the only thing my ears could hear was Mum and Mrs Pike talking and talking and talking.

The first thing I wrote down in my notebook was the registration number of a suspicious van. I'm not sure what was inside the van, but the doors at the back were tied together with extremely suspicious-looking string.

Then I saw a man with a suspicious tattoo. So I wrote down a description of him and tried to draw a picture of his tattoo. But every time Mrs Pike went round a bend, I went wrong.

Actually I didn't go wrong, my pen did. Because it wasn't a proper police pen. Proper police pens have fast ink in them that's specially designed for going around bends.

I only had a normal pen. Which was a bit of a nuisance really because I had loads of things that I needed to draw.

Everywhere I looked I saw more and more suspicious things:

By the time we got home, my notebook had almost run out of pages!

CHAPTER 18

As soon as I got in, I ran into the lounge and pushed an armchair over to the window. After all, if I was going to be the full-time eyes and ears of the community, I would need a comfy chair to sit on!

Trouble is, Mum and Mrs Pike came into the lounge just after me, with a bottle of wine and some crisps.

Then they started talking and talking and talking again!

And laughing and laughing and laughing. Which made it really hard for me to concentrate properly with either my eyes OR my ears!!

So I asked them to shhh.

The **trouble with asking my mum and Mrs Pike to shhh** is I didn't have to be a detective to know exactly what my mum was going to say next.

Especially as it had just gone eight o'clock.

"TIME FOR BED."

The **trouble with going to bed at eight o'clock in the summer** is it's FAR TOO LIGHT!

When I reminded my mum that burglars do their burgling under the cover of darkness, not the cover of lightness, she said that if I cleaned my teeth and washed my face properly, I could be the eyes and ears of the community until half past eight.

But only because she didn't have time to read me a bedtime story and because Mrs Pike was waiting for her downstairs.

So I didn't say any more about lightness and darkness after that. I put my bean bag by my window instead.

The **trouble with bean bags** is the first time you put your bottom on them, you kind of slide all over the place; especially if you've got a pen in one hand and your crime detection notebook in the other.

But after I'd wiggled my bottom around a bit and got comfortable, I had a really good view of my street from my bedroom window.

The first place I looked was the house across the road. Because if the family who lived there had gone on holiday, then this was definitely my best chance of seeing a burglar under the cover of lightness. Trouble is, there was no sign of any burglars at all. There weren't even any birds in their front garden.

So decided to look at other things instead.

The first car to drive past my house was a red one. It didn't really look that suspicious, but I wrote down its number plate in my notebook anyway – just in case it was a suspicious car disguised as a not suspicious one.

The next thing I saw was a blackbird. But it didn't look very suspicious.

Then I saw a man come out and mow his lawn. But that didn't look very suspicious either.

Then I saw a pizza being delivered further up the road, which could have looked a little bit suspicious, except I recognized the man who drove the moped because he's delivered pizzas to our house before.

The next car to drive past my house was a bit more suspicious, because it had smoke coming out of its exhaust pipe. At first I thought the smoke was probably petrol fumes, but then I realized it might be sleeping gas instead. So I wrote down the number plate of that car. Plus a description of the person who was driving it.

But after that, everything I could see with my eyes looked not very suspicious at all really.

Even when I opened my bedroom window so I could listen to the sounds outside, everything I could hear with my ears sounded not very suspicious either.

That's the **trouble with the street that I live in**: nothing very exciting ever happens in it.

CHAPTER 19

When my mum came back upstairs at 8.30, I couldn't believe half an hour had gone so quickly! My eyes and ears had only just got started! Plus it was still light outside.

When I told her that I needed more time to sit on my bean bag and watch the community and that I would go to bed when I was ready, she said I was ready for bed now.

Which wasn't the slightest bit true.

But she still drew my curtains.

And gave me a kiss.
And went downstairs.

The **trouble with Mum drawing my curtains** is it made my bedroom go really dark.

The **trouble with Mum going downstairs** is it made me feel a little bit alone.

And a little bit afraid. So I put my head under my covers.

The **trouble with putting my head under my covers** is it made things go even darker. Plus it made my imagination start imagining what would happen if the burglars came to my house for real . . . TONIGHT!

In the car on the way home from the Crimestoppers meeting, my mum had told Mrs Pike there was absolutely no way on earth that burglars would ever burgle our house, because we didn't have anything in our house that was worth stealing.

But I knew that wasn't true. I could think of loads of things that a burglar would want to steal if they came to my house FOR REAL, TONIGHT.

Like my light-up yo-yo.

And my best teddy.

And my Beyblades.

And my new colouring set.

Mum had told Mrs Pike that she could leave all the doors and windows of our house wide open all night and a burglar still wouldn't bother coming. Which wasn't true either. Plus, it suddenly made me remember . . .

The window in my bedroom was still open!

The **trouble with your bedroom window still being open** is it means burglars can get in if you don't close it.

The **trouble with closing windows when there are burglars around** is when you pull back your curtains, a burglar might be standing on a ladder outside, waiting to grab you!

The **trouble with being captured by burglars** is they will steal all your favourite toys, plus they might tie you to a chair and make you eat peas with a spoon!

So in the end I decided I would definitely have to get out of bed and close my window.

With the help of my second favourite teddy.

The **trouble with closing your bedroom window with the help of your second favourite teddy** is you still have to go with him. Because second favourite teddies can't walk. Or reach through the curtains to close a window.

The good thing though is if there is a burglar outside your window waiting to grab you, your second favourite teddy will get grabbed instead of you!

When I got to the curtains, I was almost pooing myself, I was so scared.

But luckily, when I poked my teddy's arm through the curtains and touched the window, nothing happened at all.

Even when I used teddy's paw to shut the window, nothing happened.

Which meant there can't have been any burglars hiding outside. Because if there were any burglars hiding outside they would have grabbed my teddy!

But they didn't.

So there weren't.

Which meant I had no reason to be scared at all . . .

Until I peeped out through my curtains.

When I peeped out through my curtains, I suddenly started feeling scared all over again.

Because the light outside wasn't anywhere near as light as it was before. In fact, the light outside had almost turned to dark.

So almost dark that the streetlights had come on.

Which meant the shadows had started to come out too.

Which meant that any moment now, everything outside my house would be . . . gulp . . .

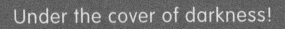

Under the cover of darkness!

CHAPTER 20

After I'd run back to my bed and got right down under my covers again, I started to think even more about all the things a burglar might want to steal from my bedroom. Like my three-colour torch or my roller blades or my box of seashells!!!

The more I thought about it, the more I realized that my house was EXACTLY the kind of house a burglar would want to burgle for real, TONIGHT!

Then I had an even worse thought!

What if the burglars had gone to the Crimestoppers meeting that evening?! What if they'd disguised themselves as English people and sat right up close to me, Gabby and Dylan?

If they had, they would have seen our crime detection notebook! And our magnifying glass. Plus they would have heard me telling

Sergeant Pennick about all the clues we'd found!

If the burglars had heard about all our clues, then they would know for sure that we were on their trail!

Then I had an even worse thought!

What if they'd followed Mrs Pike's car home after the Crimestoppers meeting?

What if they knew where I lived? If they knew where I lived, they would know how to capture me, and where to steal my crime detection notebook from!

What if they were coming to steal

our notebook TONIGHT? As well as my light-up yo-yo, my best teddy, my Beyblades, my new colouring set, three-colour torch, roller blades and seashells!

I know it sounds strange, but there was only one thing I could think of to do . . .

Borrow a packet of Doritos.

CHAPTER 21

The **trouble with borrowing a packet of Doritos** is it's better not to ask first if you're meant to be in bed. Because your mum might think you want to eat them.

It's better just to creep out of bed, creep downstairs, creep into the kitchen, borrow them really quietly and then creep back upstairs to your bedroom again.

Luckily Mum and Mrs Pike were so busy talking and talking and talking, they didn't notice me creep past the lounge door. Or creep back.

It wasn't until about five past ten that Mum finally noticed they were missing. She wouldn't have noticed at all if Mrs Pike hadn't needed to go to the loo.

The **trouble with Mrs Pike needing to go to the loo** is she had to walk past my bedroom to get to it.

Which is why she started treading on all the Doritos.

The **trouble with treading on a Dorito** is it makes a really loud crunch.

The **trouble with treading on loads of Doritos** is it makes loads of really loud crunches. Plus it makes the person who's doing all the crunching go back downstairs and tell my mum.

When Mum came up the stairs and found Doritos sprinkled all over the landing carpet, she made some really loud noises of her own.

Then, when she found Doritos all over my bedroom carpet too, she went totally doolally.

When I told her that the burglars would be trying to steal my crime detection notebook tonight, and that I needed to be able to hear their crunches when they came, she said if she heard me mention burglars one more time today, she would ground me for the rest of the summer holidays.

She said that the chances of a burglar burgling our house were rarer than an egg hatching into an elephant, and there was absolutely no need or excuse whatsoever for covering our carpets with Doritos or pickled onions or marbles or trip wires or ANYTHING!

So would I please go to SLEEP!

So I said I would.

. . .

. . .

. . .

But I couldn't.

Because I couldn't stop thinking about burglars.

The **trouble with thinking about burglars** is the harder you try not to think about them, the more you do.

I was still thinking about burglars when Mrs Pike went home. Which was at about eleven o'clock!

I was still thinking about burglars when Mum turned all the downstairs lights off.

Which was at about quarter past eleven!

The **trouble with Mum turning off all the lights downstairs** is when she did, the house got REALLY, REALLY DARK.

Darker than the cover of darkness even!

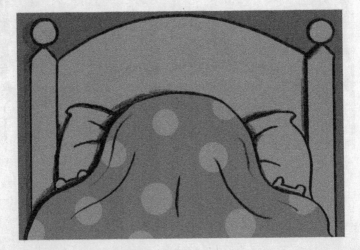

And then, when I closed my eyes really tight, it got even darker still!

When my mum came into my bedroom to check that I was asleep, I decided to make her think I was, because I didn't want to be grounded.

But I wasn't. Because no one could possibly get to sleep if they knew there were burglars around.

No one could possibly just go upstairs, go to the loo, go to the bathroom, wash their face, clean their teeth, get into bed and fall straight to sleep if they knew there were burglars around.

Except my mum!!!!

CHAPTER 22

I could not believe it when Mum started snoring!

Not just small snores either. Great big hippopotamus snores!!!

She'd only been in bed about two minutes and she was already fast asleep! I'd been in bed about three hours and I was still wide awake!

When I realized that my mum was asleep but I wasn't, the house seemed to get even darker still!

And quieter.

And shadowier.

I started to see shadows moving around in my bedroom.

Which was scary.

I started to see dark shapes over by my curtains.

Which was even scarier.

But then, just when my eyes were starting to get a bit tired, the scariest thing of all happened!

It was scarier than a shadow . . .

It was scarier than a shape . . .

It was the sound . . .

of a

creaking

gate!!!

The **trouble with hearing the sound of a creaking gate at half past eleven at night** is it makes your pyjamas go all tingly.

Especially when the gate is creaking right outside your house!

At first I thought it was the gate of my house that must be opening! But then I remembered we didn't have a gate. Because it had fallen off the other day when I was swinging on it.

Which meant it must have been somebody else's gate instead!

But whose creaking gate was it? And why was it creaking open under the cover of darkness at 11.30 at night?

By the time I had crept all the way over to my bedroom curtains, I was almost trembling!

By the time I felt brave enough to peep through the curtains and look outside, I was almost shaking.

But when I looked across the road, I nearly died of shock!

Because there, in the orangy streetlight, creeping creepily around the windows of the house on the opposite side of the road, was a human shadow! Not just a human shadow either; a human shadow with an actual torch!

The **trouble with seeing a human shadow with an actual torch** is it makes you nearly poo yourself!

And run into your mum's bedroom. "Mum, MUM! WAKE UP!" I said. "There's a burglar trying to break into the house across the road!"

The **trouble with trying to wake your mum up when she's snoring like a hippopotamus** is it's really hard.

The **trouble with trying to wake your mum up when she's snoring like a dinosaur** is it's absolutely impossible.

So I had to take charge myself!

The **trouble with taking charge yourself** is at first you're not quite sure what to do.

When I ran back into my bedroom and peeped through the curtains again, I knew I had to do something, and FAST! Because the torch beam was shining all over the house across the road now.

When it turned and flashed in my direction, I closed the peephole in my curtains tight.

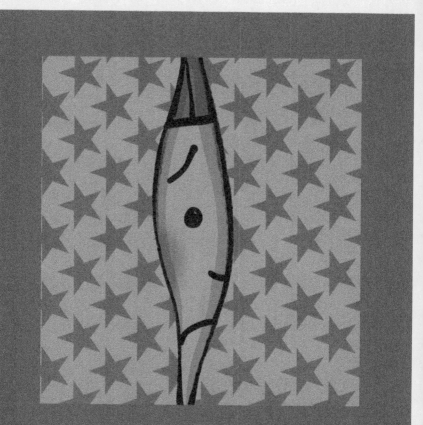

But even through the tiniest of gaps I could still see what the shadowy figure was doing. He was looking for a way to get in!

He was shining
his torch along the
downstairs window
ledges and all over

the lock on the front
door, including
the letterbox!

And the front step. And the flower pots!

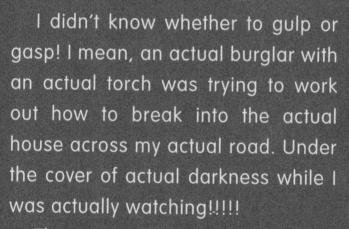

I didn't know whether to gulp or gasp! I mean, an actual burglar with an actual torch was trying to work out how to break into the actual house across my actual road. Under the cover of actual darkness while I was actually watching!!!!!

There was only one thing I could do. I had to call the police right away!

The **trouble with calling the police right away** is I needed to use the house phone.

The **trouble with using the house phone** is it meant I needed to go downstairs!

On my own.
In the DARK DARK!!
UNDER THE COVER
OF DARKNESS!!

I wanted to turn the lights on, but then I realized that if the burglar saw the lights in my house go on, he would probably run away.

So I kept the lights off, did a gulp and a gasp, grabbed my first and second favourite teddies and went downstairs in the dark dark on my own.

The **trouble with ringing 999** is I've never done it before.

Which meant that as soon as the 999 lady answered, I tried to tell her everything really, really fast.

"QUICK! THERE'S A BURGLAR TRYING TO BREAK INTO THE HOUSE ACROSS THE ROAD AND HE'S ARMED WITH A TORCH AND HE MIGHT HAVE A GUN AND I THINK HE MIGHT BE RUSSIAN AND HE MIGHT HAVE A LIMP, BUT HE'S DEFINITELY GOT SHADOWS, AND IF YOU DON'T COME QUICK, HE'LL STEAL ALL THE THINGS OUT OF THE HOUSE BECAUSE THE PEOPLE WHO LIVE THERE ARE ON HOLIDAY, AND IF YOU DON'T COME AND CATCH HIM FAST, HE MIGHT BURGLE ME NEXT BECAUSE I'VE GOT LOADS OF THINGS WORTH BURGLING, PLUS MY MUM'S ASLEEP SO SHE WON'T HEAR ANYTHING IF I GET CAPTURED AND HE FORCES ME TO EAT PEAS!"

The **trouble with saying everything too fast** is the 999 lady makes you stop and take a deep, deep breath, then say everything all over again, only really slowly.

Plus, you first of all have to tell her your name and where you live, plus you need to tell her the address of the house that the burglar is burgling.

Which makes you really desperate, because if you're doing everything slowly, the burglar might be getting away!

When the police cars screeched into our road with their blue lights flashing and their sirens sirening, things got really exciting! In fact, things got so exciting, loads of people who lived in our road came out in their dressing gowns to see what was happening!

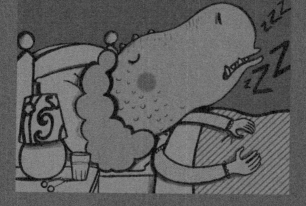

Mum didn't. She was still snoring like a dinosaur. And dribbling.

As soon as the police cars screeched to a stop outside the house across the road, about six policemen jumped out, raced through the creaky gate, and then bombed straight down the path and into the house through the open front door!

About eight and a half seconds later, six policemen dragged the burglar out of the house, through the creaky gate, and held him up under the streetlights.

That's when I closed my curtains really quickly.

Because that's when I realized

it wasn't a burglar at all.
Or even a him.
It was Mrs Pike.
With handcuffs on.

CHAPTER 23

The **trouble with people knocking on your door at twenty to twelve at night** is you really don't want to answer it.

Especially if you know that the person knocking is a policeman.

So I didn't answer it.

I pretended there was no one in.

But after about twenty-seven knocks and quite a few shouts through our letterbox, I decided that I really would have to wake my mum.

So I did.

The **trouble with throwing a glass of water over your mum's face** is it doesn't just wake her up, it makes her quite wet too.

And spluttery.

When I told her that there was someone knocking on our front door and I thought it might be a policeman, I don't think she really understood what I was saying.

Which is probably why she forgot to put on her dressing gown.

When she opened the door and found Mrs Pike standing on our doorstep, wearing proper metal handcuffs and standing next to a policeman with a very serious face, all she could do was stare.

The policeman told my mum that Mrs Pike claimed to be our neighbour and said she had been asked by the people who lived across the road to feed their cat while they were away on holiday.

Mrs Pike then said that she had had trouble finding the key with her torch, but when she had found the key and finally got into the kitchen, she had been jumped on by six police officers.

Apparently cat biscuits had gone everywhere.

Which was bad.

But then things got worse.

Because then the policeman told my mum that it was me who had rung the police in the first place.

Which meant it was me who had got Mrs Pike handcuffed. And me who had woken everyone in the street.

At first I thought Mum might be too tired to get too cross with me, but I think making her wet three times in one day might have helped to wake her up.

"WHY DIDN'T YOU WAKE ME EARLIER, DAISY?" she shouted. "IF YOU'D WOKEN ME UP EARLIER INSTEAD OF CALLING THE POLICE, ALL THIS SILLY BURGLAR NONSENSE COULD HAVE BEEN AVOIDED!"

When I said I couldn't wake her up because she was snoring like a dinosaur, she got even crosser!

Then, when I told the policeman that she had been drinking wine with Mrs Pike and that when my mum drinks wine she always snores like a dinosaur, her eyes nearly popped out of her head she was so cross.

Luckily, because the policeman was standing on the doorstep, she couldn't shout at me any louder. So she sent me to my room instead.

Trouble is, just as I was about to go up the stairs, another policeman walked down our garden path and

asked my mum about the car that was parked outside our house.

When the policeman told my mum that he'd noticed our car didn't have any car tax, she said she was very sorry and that she would do something about it first thing in the morning.

Then she said she hadn't been driving her car since her car tax had run out.

But I remembered that she had. So I reminded her about her trip to Ikea. And all the other places she'd been to.

I'm not sure whose face turned crossest after that – my mum's or the policeman's.

Half an hour later, our car got picked up and towed away by a special police pick-up lorry with flashing orange lights. I watched it all happen from my bean bag, before my mum came back into my bedroom and took my bean bag away.

Apparently she's going to give it to a charity shop. And if I don't start behaving myself, she's going to give me to a charity shop too.

GULP!

I've decided not to be a detective any more.

DAISY'S
TROUBLE
INDEX

The trouble with . . .

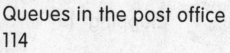

To Santa

DAISY

and the TROUBLE with

CHRISTMAS

by Kes Gray

RED FOX

CHAPTER 1

The **trouble with Christmas** is it's
tOOOOOOOOOOOOOOOOOOOOOOOO
OOOOOOOOOOOOOOOOOOOOOOOO
OOOOOOOOOOOOOOOOOOOOOOOO
OOOOOOOOOOOOOOOOOOOOOOOO
OOOOOOOOOOOOOOOOOOOOOOOO
OOOOOOOOOOOOOOOOOOOOOOOO
OOOOOOOOOOOOOOOOOOOOOOOO
OOOOOOOOOOOOOOOOOOOOOOOO
OOOOOOOOOOOOOOOOOOOOOOOO
OOOOOOOOOOOOOOOOOOOOOOOO
OOOOOOOOOOOOOOOOOOOOOOOO
OOOOOOOOOOOOOOOOOOOOOOOO

OOOOOOOOOOOOOOOOOOOOOOOOOO
OOOOOOOOOOOOOOOOOOOOOOOOOO
OOOOOOOOOOOOOOOOOOOOOOOOOO
OOOOOOOOOOOOOOOOOOOOOOOOOO
OOOOOOOOOOOOOOOOOOOOOOOOOO
OOOOOOOOOOOOOOOOOOOOOOOOOO
OOOOOOOOOOOOOOOOOOOOOOOOOO
OOOOOOOOOOOOOOOOOOOOOOOOOO
OOOOOOOOOOOOOOOOOOOOOOOOOO
OOOOOOOOOOOOOOOOOOOOOOOOOO
OOOOOOOOOOOOOOOOOOOOOOOOOO
EXCITING!!!!!!!!!!!!!!!!!!!!!!!!!!!!!!!!!!!!!!
!!!!!!!!!!!!!

If Christmas wasn't sooooooooooo
ooooooooooooooooooooooooooooooo
ooooooooooooooooooooooooooooooo
ooooooooooooooooooooooooooooooo
ooooooooooooooooooooooooooooooo
ooooooooooooooooooooooooooooooo
ooooooooooooooooooooooooooooooo
oooooooooooooo exciting, then what
happened in the school Christmas
play this afternoon would never have
happened in the first place.

WHICH ISN'T MY FAULT!!!!!!!!!!!!!!!!
!!!!!!!!!!!!!!!!!!!!!!!!!!!!!!

Ask Gabby. Ask Paula Potts. Ask
anyone who isn't Mrs Peters, or any
of the other teachers, or my mum or

Gabby's mum and dad!

It's all Christmas's fault. Not mine. If Christmas hadn't made me get so excited, then everything would have been just fine.

Except it wasn't fine.

It was a bit embarrassing really.

CHAPTER 2

The trouble with Christmas excitement is it gets you all over.

It goes into your toes and your fingers and your elbows and your hair and your eyeballs and up your jumper. It wiggles into your brain through your ears. It gets you in your lips so you can't stop smiling. It gets you in your

legs so you can't stop skipping.

It gets you inside your tummy so your heartbeat won't stop going *bibbidy-bibbidy-bop* ALL the time. It even gets you in your eyelashes, so you can't close your eyes properly when you go to bed.

And it lasts for AGES!

My Christmas excitement started in September!

September is when all the Christmassy things come into the shops. My mum says it's a disgrace putting Christmassy things in the shops in September. My mum says that shops should only put their

Christmassy things on the shelves in about November when it's nearly Christmas, not September when it's still nearly summer.

But I think she's wrong. I think shops should get rid of all their normal things

(apart from sweets) in about January, and then have Christmassy things on their shelves until Christmas.

I LOVE Christmassy things! In fact when I'm about twenty-seven that's what I'm going to be; a Christmassy-thing shop owner! Who only sells Christmassy things!

Unless Santa gives me a job, that is.

The **trouble with Santa** is you never get to actually see him.

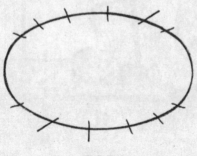

Even when he comes down the chimney with all your presents, you won't see him. That's because he magicks you asleep before he comes.

Did you know that when Santa touches the side of his nose with his finger, it makes him small enough to go up and down chimneys? It's true because I've seen it in a book. You will never ever get to see the real Santa because his magic is so good.

You can still write to him though. I wrote a letter to Santa in October. It said:

To Santa
Santa's House
The North Pole

Dear Santa,

Please when I grow up can
I be one of your helpers?
I will try not to grow up too
much because I know elves
are usually very short, but I'm
really good at wrapping presents,
plus I can bring my own red
scissors, plus I would be really
good at feeding Rudolph.
So please can I have a job
when I'm about seventeen?

Love,
Daisy

The **trouble with writing letters** to Santa is they have to be sent to the North Pole, which is the farthest away place in the world.

The **trouble with walking to the North Pole** is it will really make your postman's feet ache.

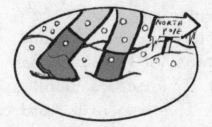

My mum says the quickest way to send a letter to Santa is to magic it there. I thought she was going to say by hovercraft or something, but she didn't. She said if I gave my letter to her on Bonfire Night, she would post it for me then.

So I did. Plus I wrote my Christmas list to Santa too!

Dear Santa,
I know it isn't even December yet, but my mum says she's going to magic my letter and my Christmas list to you on Bonfire Night. In case you didn't know, I've been really good all year. Well, nearly all year.

And when I wasn't that good, it wasn't my fault! So please can I have these things for my Christmas presents:

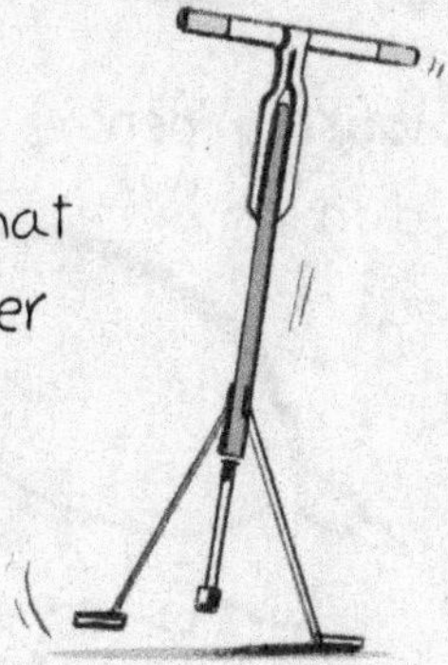

· pogo stick that doesn't fall over

· skateboard with engine

· yoyo that does tricks

· colouring pencils
that don't snap

· colouring pens
that don't
run out

· red and white football
that scores goals

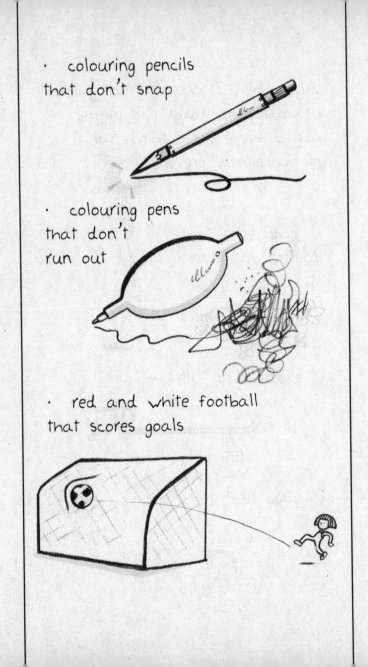

- quite a fluffy hamster

- bike that fires torpedoes

- bubble bath that makes the water green

- craft scissors with pointy ends

- worm house with real worms · big cactus

- chocolate money (or real money to buy chocolate money)

- skipping rope long enough for about twenty people

· super Soaker water pistol with about ten different action squirts

· new watch

PS. If you run out of room on your sleigh, can I definitely have the bike that fires torpedoes first?

Love,
Daisy

xxxxxxxxxxxxxxxxxxxxxxxxxxxx

When my mum read my Christmas list, she said Santa didn't make bikes with torpedoes. Then she said that I would need to be on my very best behaviour right up to Christmas Day if I was going to get even half of the things I'd written down.

So I promised I wouldn't get into even the slightest bit of trouble.

Not before Christmas. Not during Christmas. Not even after Christmas.

I was doing really, really well – until today.

Sighhhhhh.

I do hope Santa wasn't watching the school Christmas play this afternoon.

CHAPTER 3

Before I tell you about what happened at the school Christmas play today, I must tell you what happened on Bonfire Night in November.

I love Bonfire Night, don't you?

When we went to the bonfire party, there were loads of people everywhere. Everyone had wellington boots on, and lots of people were holding sparklers! It was really exciting! (Not as exciting as Christmas though.) Plus there was the hugest bonfire in the world! It was so big,

I could feel how hot it was even when I was standing a really long way away!

That's the **trouble with bonfires** – you mustn't ever go anywhere near them because they might set you alight. Or make your wellingtons melt off.

In the field where the bonfire was I couldn't see any letter boxes at all. It was very dark because it was night time, but I was sure there was nowhere I could post my Christmas letter to Santa. But Mum said she wouldn't need a post box or a postman to post my Christmas list – she would need a man in a yellow jacket.

Men in yellow jackets are called "marshals". Their job is to let off all the fireworks on Bonfire Night, and to make sure no one gets too close to the bonfire.

Their other job is to send Christmas letters to Santa!

The marshal who my mum spoke to looked really kind. After my mum had whispered in his ear, he smiled at me and asked me for my Santa letters.

So I gave them to him.
And then guess what he did!
He put them on the bonfire!!!

At first I didn't understand. But Mum told me that bonfire magic would send all the words on my letters right up into the air, through the clouds and past the stars, all the way to Santa's home.

Just like that!

She said if I watched the bonfire carefully I would see the words from other children's Santa letters whizzing up into the sky!

And she was right! There were loads of sparks flying up from the bonfire all over the place!

I saw all the words I'd written to Santa fly right up into the sky –

Santa, reindeer, pogo stick, bike and *torpedo* – glowing really orange before they went black and disappeared. It was brilliant!

Mum said she was absolutely sure that Santa would get my Christmas letter and my Christmas list. Which made me even more excited!

All I had to do now was wait for Christmas!

CHAPTER 4

The **trouble with November** is it's got thirty days in it. If November only had one day in it, it wouldn't have gone so slowly.

I've now been waiting forty-one and a half days since Bonfire Night, but there are still nine more days to go till Christmas Day!

Oh, I do wish Christmas would hurry up!

The **trouble with waiting for Christmas** is it even makes the bits of you that don't usually get excited get really excited too!

This morning when I was getting dressed, even my school socks felt excited!

Then, when I tried on my school play costume this morning, I got excited tingles all over!

The school Christmas play happened this afternoon.

Kind of.

I couldn't wait for it to start.

Trouble is, then I couldn't wait for it to end.

Because it all went wrong.

Very wrong, actually.

Mum says things wouldn't have gone wrong at all if I hadn't got myself so excited. Gabby said that when it all went wrong, it was really funny and all my friends thought it was really funny too.

But Mrs Peters, my teacher, said

I had let myself down, my class down, the school down and everyone in the audience down too.

Oooh dear. I hope I haven't let Santa down!

And anyway, it wasn't my fault!

It was Mrs Peters' fault.

It wasn't me who told me to be in the school Christmas play today.

It was Mrs Peters.

It wasn't me who told me to carry the baby Jesus over to Mary today.

It was Mrs Peters.

And it wasn't me who told me to cradle and rock the baby Jesus before I handed him over to Mary today.

It was Mrs Peters.

So if anyone should be in for it, it shouldn't be me.

It should be MRS PETERS!

In fact it should be Mrs Peters who has to go and see the headmaster at nine o'clock tomorrow morning.

NOT ME!

CHAPTER 5

It was about three weeks ago that Mrs Peters told my class we were going to be doing a school Christmas play.

She clapped her hands after our spelling test, and said the lower school Christmas play was going to be in the afternoon, on Wednesday 16 December.

I was feeling a bit cross when she told us, because I'd just spelled poison with a P-O-Y.

And an S-E-N.

That's the **trouble with spellings**.
My mum doesn't make me practise
them enough.

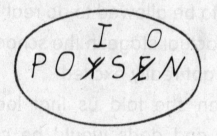

Anyway, I cheered up straight away
when I heard the exciting news!

When it was last year's Christmas
play, my class only sat and watched.

And clapped.

That's because we weren't old
enough to be the actual people in
the actual play.

But this year we were old enough and big enough and everything!

When Mrs Peters told us we were going to be allowed to do real acting on an actual stage in the school hall, we all got really excited!

When she told us that loads of mums and dads would be coming to watch us too, Fiona Tucker nearly wet herself!

That's the **trouble with Fiona Tucker**. She drinks too much fruit juice at lunch time.

Mrs Peters said that doing a Christmas play would mean lots of hard work and rehearsals. Rehearsals means practising with your teacher or your mum to make sure you're doing the acting right.

She said we would have to learn our lines and lots of new songs as well. Plus we would all have to make our own outfits!

Well, our mums would.

Then Mrs Peters said that the very next day she would be telling everyone in the class what person in the Christmas play they were going to be.

I put my hand up straight away to ask if I could be the three king with the gold, but Mrs Peters told everyone to put their hands down.

Mrs Peters said she would let everybody know who they were going to be after assembly the next morning. Then she gave us a school newsletter to take home.

When Gabby and me met my mum outside the school gates, my mum read the special Christmas newsletter and said, "How lovely! I do so love the story of Christmas! I wonder what carols you'll sing. I wonder what roles you and Gabby are going to play."

I said there weren't any rolls in the story of Christmas.

Then my mum said, "Not bread rolls, Daisy, roles roles. A role is a part; a part is the person you are going to be acting in the play."

I said I wanted to be the three king with the gold, because then I'd be rich! Gabby said she wanted to be a Mary with a blue dress, because she already had a blue dress in her wardrobe at home.

Then me and Gabby got so excited, we made up a special Christmas game to play all the way home from school.

In our game, you both take turns to think of something Christmassy that you love! The first person who can't think of a Christmassy thing that they absolutely love loses the game.

Except it's impossible to lose, because there are *so* many things at Christmas that are so loverlyloverlyloverly!!!

"I love Santa!" I said.

And Gabby said she loved Santa too!

"I love snowmen!" said Gabby.
And I said I loved snowmen too!!

Then I said I loved Christmas
presents!
And Gabby said she loved
Christmas presents too!!!

"I love Christmas stockings!" said Gabby.

"I love being in a Christmas school play!" I said. "Especially if I'm going to be a three king!"

But then, without even asking, my mum joined in our special Christmas game.

"I love Christmas carols!" she said.

Trouble is, then she actually started singing one too . . .

The **trouble with my mum singing Christmas carols** is she can't sing. In fact my mum sounds really weird when she sings, or even hums.

So Gabby and me had to stop playing our special Christmas game after that. We had to walk with our hands over our ears, all the way home from school.

CHAPTER 6

When I called for Gabby the next morning, my whole school uniform felt excited! Not only was I going to be acting in a school Christmas play, but Gabby's mum and dad had made Gabby's front garden into the most Christmassy front garden in the whole world!

They'd put a big dancing snowman by the wheelie bin, and a light-up Rudolph with a flashing red nose on the lawn, plus loads of other really good Christmassy things,

PLUS Christmas lights stretching right round all the windows of the whole house!!!

My mum says that Gabby's house always looks "a bit tacky" at Christmas ("tacky" means not that good), but she's definitely wrong. Gabby's Christmas garden decorations are totally brilliant. I wish I had a plastic reindeer with a flashing nose on my lawn.

And a blow-up sleigh with real sleigh-bell sounds, on my roof.

And a blow-up Santa that says *Ho-ho-ho.*

And plastic dancing elves that go *Hee-hee-hee* when you walk past them!

After I'd knocked on Gabby's door, I patted Rudolph on the head, said *Ho-ho-ho* to Santa, *Hee-hee-hee* to the elves, and then stood back on the path to look at the Christmas tree in Gabby's lounge window.

Gabby's Christmas tree is really beautiful. It's made of actual tree and it's got decorations and tinsel all over it. And it's got flashing lights. Gabby's Christmas tree lights are red and green and yellow and blue, and they do three speeds of flashing!

My mum thinks Gabby's Christmas tree lights are a bit tacky too.

But I REALLY like them!

PLUS Gabby's mum and dad leave their Christmas tree lights on all day! In my house we only have our Christmas tree lights on when it gets dark. Because my mum says we need to save on electricity.

The **trouble with saving on electricity** is Christmas lights don't look quite as good when they're switched off.

They still look quite good, but when the lights on our tree are switched on they sparkle really bright and white. Our Christmas tree lights at home look just like twinkling fairies when they are switched on. Which is just as good as coloured flashing lights.

The **trouble with our Christmas tree at home** is it's a bit wonky. That's because Mum keeps bending it when she puts it back up in the loft.

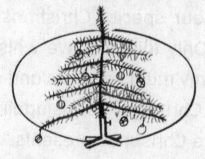

Our Christmas tree is made of green plastic, and it's got branches that you have to screw on. When it's just been screwed together, it doesn't look very good, but once we've put all the decorations on and got the lights to work, it looks really brilliant.

If I could swap Gabby's Christmas tree for my Christmas tree, I would. But I think I would probably keep my lights.

On the way to school Gabby and me played our special Christmas game again! Only this time we whispered, in case my mum heard us and started singing Christmas carols again.

"I love Christmas presents,"

 whispered Gabby.

"We said that yesterday!" I laughed.

"But I really do, though!" laughed Gabby.

"I love snow!" whispered Gabby.

"I love snow too," whispered me.

"Apart from when it goes all slushy."

"I love throwing snowballs!" said Gabby.

"Me too!" said me.

"I love Christmas cards!" said Gabby.

"I love Christmas decorations!" said me.

"I love mince pies!" said Gabby.

"I love Christmas cake!" said me.

"I love turkey!" said Gabby.

"I love stuffing!" said me.

"I love Christmas carols!" said my mum again!

And then *guess what*? She started singing Christmas carols again!

So we had to stop playing our special Christmas game AGAIN!

And listen to my mum all the way to the school.

I nearly didn't give her a kiss at the school gates, her singing was so terrible.

CHAPTER 7

When we got into school, everyone in the whole playground was really, really excited about being in a school Christmas play!

Colin Kettle wanted to be a shepherd, Nishta Baghwat wanted to be an angel with at least six wings, Paula Potts wanted to be a three king but didn't mind which present she brought, and Liam Chaldecott's dad said if Liam wasn't Joseph he was going to write to Mrs Peters to complain.

In assembly, Gabby and me were so excited we could only pretend to sing the songs, our voices had gone so squeaky!

Harry Bayliss fidgeted all the way through because he wanted to be a Roman soldier with an actual sword. Fiona Tucker nearly wet herself again because she was bursting to be an angel with a magic wand. And Liberty Pearce said she had done a prayer to God asking if she could have first ride on the camels.

"I sooooooo hope I'm the three king with the gold!" I said to Gabby as we walked back to our classroom.

"And I sooooooooooooooooooooooo hope I'm Mary," said Gabby.

Gabby said that Mary was the best person to be in the Christmas play by faaaaaar, because you got to wear a blue dress. (Gabby's favourite colour is blue.) Plus she said Mary can ride donkeys sideways.

I told her only circus people can ride donkeys sideways, but Gabby said she had seen a photo of Mary actually doing it. So it must be true.

I told Gabby that even if Mary could ride donkeys sideways, we weren't allowed alive donkeys in the school play, plus the three king with the gold had a camel, and camels were much better than donkeys.

Double plus, wearing a gold crown was much better than wearing a blue cloak.

And carrying a golden present was even better!

Then I said there was no way Gabby was going to be Mary anyway, because she had blonde hair.

So then Gabby got a bit cross, and kicked the wall in the corridor.

The **trouble with kicking walls in corridors** is it scuffs the toe of your school shoes.

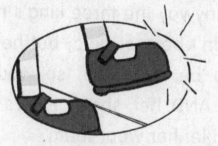

Gabby said she'd be in for it if her mum saw the scuff, because she'd only had her shoes on for two hours.

I said to spit on it when we got back to the classroom and then rub it with her finger. That always makes my scuffs go away. At least for a while.

Then Gabby said she would wear a black Mary wig if she had to, plus we weren't allowed alive camels either, and anyway the three king's present wouldn't be real gold, but her cloak would be real blue, so would her hood AND her shoes if Mrs Peters would let her wear them.

That's the **trouble with blue school shoes**. They have to be black.

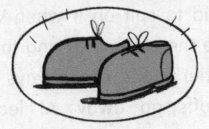

Otherwise you get told off.

Especially if they're white trainers.

CHAPTER 8

When we got back to our classroom after assembly, and sat down at our desks, Mrs Peters had to clap her hands SIX TIMES before she could get everyone to be quiet. Then she had to clap AGAIN, because Jack Beechwhistle STILL wouldn't be quiet.

Then Fiona Tucker put her hand up and asked if she could go to the loo, so we had to wait even longer to find out which person in the Christmas play we were going to be.

Fiona Tucker must have been really really bursting, because she took absolutely ages to come back.

She took so long, Liberty Pearce had to go to the loo too!

Then Colin Kettle.

And then Jack Beechwhistle! (But he wasn't allowed, because he didn't really need to go.)

When everyone had come back from the loo, Mrs Peters clapped her hands two times more again, and said, "Right, children. Quiet please, children, while I read out my list. On this list are the names of the children in the class who I have chosen to be the lead characters in the school Christmas play. After I have read out your name, I will read out the name of the character you are going to be. For example: Gabriella, you will be Mary."

That's the **trouble with Gabby**. She's really jammy.

Once Gabby had stopped squealing like a hamster, Mrs Peters read out all the other parts in the play.

357

Daniel Carrington was going to be Joseph.

Nishta Baghwat was going to be the three king with the gold.

Vicky Carrow was going to be the three king with the frankincense. Harry Bayliss was the three king with the myrrh.

Liberty Pearce, Fiona Tucker and Jasmine Smart were all going to be angels.

 Daniel McNicholl was going to be a bright shining star.

Jack Beechwhistle was going to be King Herod.

Colin Kettle,
Sanjay Lapore
and Bernadette
Laine were all
Roman soldiers,
with ACTUAL
SWORDS.

Liam Chaldecott
was going to be
the innkeeper.

Melanie Simpson
was going to be
a barmaid.

David Alexander, Barry Morely and Stephanie Brakespeare were going to be shepherds.

Paula Potts was going to be a sheepdog.

And all the children in the class who hadn't had their names read out were going to be part of a special gang of singing sheep, called the "Woolly Wonkas".

Oh yes . . .

And I was going to be Mary's helper.

At first, when Mrs Peters told me I was going to be Mary's helper, I didn't know what to say.

Or think.

I'd heard of a Mary before, but I'd never heard of a Mary's helper.

So then I asked Gabby what it was.

"What's a Mary's helper?" I whispered.

"It's someone who helps ME!" said Gabby, all excitedly. "Isn't it good, Daisy! You and me are going to be together on stage in the school play! Mrs Peters has put us together!

Because we're best friends! Isn't it brilliant?!"

So I forgot about being a three king, and got really excited about being a Mary's helper instead!

Gabby was going to be Mary! And I was going to be her helper! We were going to be a special Christmas team together, in the school Christmas play!

How exciting was that!

CHAPTER 9

After Mrs Peters had read out all the parts that we were going to be in the Christmas play, she made us all calm down again.

Except for Jack Beechwhistle. Jack Beechwhistle wouldn't calm down at all.

He just wouldn't stop waving his arms about and asking who King Herod was. In the end he asked so much, he had to go and stand outside the classroom door!

After about five minutes, Mrs Peters let him back in.

Then she told us the story of Christmas!

The **trouble with the story of Christmas** is it's a bit strange in the beginning if you ask me.

It goes like this:

One day (actually night) Mary (who was going to be Gabby) was asleep in bed when she had a dream.

God (who wasn't going to be anyone) spoke to Mary in her dreams and told her she was going to have a baby.

Plus he told her that the baby was going to be called Jesus, and that Jesus would be his son.

But although Jesus would be God's son, God needed a different dad to look after him. So God told Mary to ask her husband, who was called Joseph, to be Jesus' dad instead.

That's the **trouble with being God**. You are far too busy to look after babies. Even if it's *your* own baby!

Then Daniel Carrington, who was going to be Joseph, put his hand up and asked Mrs Peters a question.

He said, "Missssss, if Mary is Joseph's wife but she's having God's baby, does that mean she's been having an affair?"

Mrs Peters went a bit red, and said no, it didn't. It just meant that God "moves in mysterious ways".

Then Jack Beechwhistle started moving in mysterious ways in his school chair. So he got sent out of the classroom again.

After he was let back in, Mrs Peters told us that Joseph was really pleased when he heard the news about Baby Jesus.

Joseph was a carpenter, so I reckon he probably started carving some wooden toys for baby Jesus to play with.

Then baby Jesus started growing in Mary's tummy and everyone was really happy.

Until one day, just before Jesus was going to be born, Mary and Joseph were told that they would have to go all the way to a town called Bethlehem to put their names down on a special list.

Bethlehem was the place where

Joseph and Mary were born and the special list was an "I was born here" list called a census.

The trouble with censuses is if you've moved somewhere else, you have to go all the way back straight away, even if you're going to have a baby. Otherwise you won't get on the list.

So Mary and Joseph bought a donkey to take them all the way from the town they were living in, called Nazareth, to the town they were born in, called Bethlehem.

The **trouble with donkeys** is they're not big enough for two people so Joseph had to walk all the way there.

Nishta Baghwat said they should have bought a camel instead because they're bigger, plus they can fit two people on.

But the **trouble with camels** is they are very expensive, so only three kings can afford to buy them.

So it had to be a donkey.

I don't know what the donkey was called but I would have called him Buttons.

So one warm and starry night, Mary, Joseph and Buttons set off across the desert to go to Bethlehem.

The **trouble with deserts** is all the sand looks the same, which means you can get lost really easily if you're not careful. Especially in the dark.

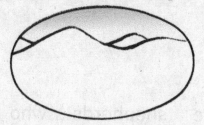

So to help Mary and Joseph find Bethlehem without getting lost, God put a great big shining star in the sky right above it.

Then some angels started telling other people to follow the star to Bethlehem too.

Some shepherds who were watching their Woolly Wonkas by night were told how special baby Jesus was going to be and where he was going to be born.

Plus three kings were told about Jesus by some other angels too.

All the kings and all the shepherds wanted to see baby Jesus being born, so off they all went to Bethlehem, with lots of sheep and presents.

Mary and Joseph got to Bethlehem first because they had a head start. Trouble is, they couldn't find anywhere to stay.

Every time they knocked at an inn, the innkeepers said they were full.

Barry Morely said the innkeepers were out of order, because they must have been able to find a space for Mary and Joseph to sleep somewhere,

even if it was on a settee. Especially if Mary was going to have a baby.

But in the end a kinder innkeeper did give Mary and Joseph somewhere to stay. He let them sleep in his stable.

The **trouble with sleeping in a stable** is it must have been really smelly.

Stables are like barns and they're full of cows and sheep and things.

Even with nice fresh straw in it, a stable would still whiff of you-know-what. Especially if a horse did a whoopsie.

But Mrs Peters said Mary and Joseph had no choice. So that is where baby Jesus was born! In a stable! With all the whiffs and whoopsies.

Paula Potts said her mum had just had a baby and if she ever had a baby too there is no way she would have it in a stable. When she had a baby she was going to have it in a nice clean hospital, and after she brought her baby home, she would give it a lovely warm cot with teddy bears in it, plus a mobile that played sleepy time tunes. PLUS she'd have a baby listening monitor and a special place for dirty nappies.

But Mrs Peters said they didn't have things like that in olden days. All Mary and Joseph had for Jesus to be born in was something called a manger. And they even had to borrow that!

The **trouble with mangers** is they aren't meant to be used for cots at all!

I mean, do you know what a manger is? It's a wooden box that you put horses' food in! You know, actual horse food, like hay and grass and sugar lumps and stuff!

There's no way you're meant to put a baby in a manger, not even if you take all the sugar lumps out first and fill it with the cleanest hay on earth. But Mary and Joseph did!

And the shepherds and the three kings let them!

If you ask me, the last thing baby Jesus needed was gold, frankincense and myrrh. He'd have been much better off with a new cot, a nice big teddy and some lovely soft blankets.

That's the **trouble with the three kings**. They went and brought the wrong presents.

After Jesus was born, all the
shepherds and the sheep and the
kings and probably some chickens
gathered round the manger to
see how special he was. He was
so special everyone said he was
going to grow up to be king of ALL

the kings in ALL the world!

Then, after that, everyone apart from Mary, Joseph and baby Jesus went home.

But that wasn't the end of the story, though! We thought it was, but it wasn't!

Because another king called Herod found out that Jesus had been born. And he wasn't happy about it at all!! In fact, he was even more jealous of Jesus than Santa's reindeers are of Rudolph!

Herod wanted himself to be king of all the kings, not Jesus, so do you know what he decided to do?

He was sooooooooo jealous, he sent all his Roman soldiers out to find Jesus. And kill him! With actual swords!!

Then the dinner bell went.

Not in Bethlehem, because Bethlehem didn't have dinner bells.

At least stables didn't.

The dinner bell went outside our classroom door.

Mrs Peters said that we didn't have to worry about Jesus over lunch because in the Bible he would be kept safe from Herod's soldiers and he would still grow up to be king of all the kings in all the world.

Which was good, because the **trouble with trying to eat your packed lunch when you're worrying about baby Jesus** is it could make it really hard for your sandwiches to go down.

So everything was all right after that.

Until Jack Beechwhistle tried to arrest us.

CHAPTER 10

The **trouble with Jack Beechwhistle being a King Herod** is he thinks it makes him the boss of the whole playground.

Which meant after lunch he was sending Colin Kettle, Sanjay Lapore and Bernadette Laine all over the place to arrest people, because he said they were his soldiers and they had to follow his orders.

But me and Gabby said there was no way King Herod was going to arrest us. Especially if he was the same person as Jack Beechwhistle.

Colin, Bernadette and Sanjay said we had to be arrested because they were soldiers. Plus they had swords.

We said we couldn't see any swords.

So they said that's because their swords were invisible. Which wasn't true, so me and Gabby told them to go away.

Then Jack Beechwhistle came over

to us and ordered us to definitely surrender to his soldiers. So we called them all poopy heads and stuck our tongues out.

The **trouble with calling soldiers poopy heads** is then they turn their invisible swords into invisible choppers. Plus King Herod switches to cosmic power!

Cosmic power is really dangerous if it touches you, so we had to run away really fast after that!

Luckily we found the three kings with presents over by the quiet area, so we got them to come and fight with us.

Jack Beechwhistle said his three soldiers were stronger than our three kings, but Harry Bayliss said his three king crown fired golden bullets!

Then Vicky Carrow changed her frankincense into poison gas, and Nishta Baghwat made her robe into a Spider-Man net!

We arrested Herod and all his soldiers after that.

SWORD POWER!

POISON GAS POWER!

LIGHTNING POWER!

SPIDER WEB POWER!

INVISIBLE POWER!

Except Jack Beechwhistle let himself out of jail straight away, because he said he was king of nearly all the land, which meant he could change the law.

And he let his soldiers out of jail too. And gave them their invisible choppers back, which was really annoying at first, but it didn't matter in the end, because lunch time was over and we had to go back to our class.

That's the **trouble with playtime bells**. They always ring when you're having the most fun.

It was only when I was walking back to class with Gabby that I suddenly realized something really important.

I'd heard the story of Christmas, but I still didn't know what a Mary's helper had to do.

After what happened in the school play this afternoon, I wish I'd never found out.

CHAPTER 11

"What do you think Mary's helper helps Mary to do?" I asked Gabby on the way back to class.

"I'm not exactly sure," said Gabby. "Maybe you could help me get on and off my donkey sideways, or perhaps you could help me tidy up the stable so it's nicer for having a baby in."

"I'm not cleaning up the cow whoopsies!" I said. "Or sheep droppings or piggy poos! No way am I helping you do that!"

Gabby laughed and said the best

thing to do was ask Mrs Peters that afternoon.

So I did. Just after singalong time.

Mrs Peters told the class that everyone would find out exactly what they had to do in the play when rehearsals started the next day. But then she said as I had sung so nicely,

she would tell me exactly what a Mary's helper had to do.

I was so excited about finding out, it was ME that nearly wet myself this time, not Fiona Tucker!

And believe me, what I had to do was REALLY, REALLY IMPORTANT!

And REALLY, REALLY, REALLY EXCITING!!!!

Mrs Peters said having a baby was a very tiring thing to do, so once Mary had put the newborn baby Jesus in the manger, I would have to come in and help!

I would need to take the newborn baby Jesus away from Mary, wash him, bathe him and give him some clean clothes.

Mrs Peters said that when I took the baby Jesus away, the lights on the stage would go out, everything in the stable would go dark, and everyone, including the Woolly Wonkas, would sing a Christmas celebration song. (Mary and me wouldn't have to sing though, because Mary would be too busy resting and I would be too busy helping.)

Then, when the lights came back on, I would need to bring the baby Jesus back to Mary, all clean and dressed and lovely.

Plus, before I gave him back to Mary I had to cradle and rock him!

DOUBLE PLUS, you'll never guess what!

I had to say a whole line of words all by myself too!

"BEHOLD! THE KING OF KINGS IS BORN!"

I had to say ALL of that, in my really loudest voice! ALL by myself!

Do you know how many words that is that I had to learn?

SEVEN WHOLE WORDS!!!!!!! ALLLLL to myself!

PLUS PLUS PLUS!!!

I even had to remember to do a

curtsey too, before I gave baby Jesus back to Mary – I mean Gabby – I mean Mary!

Well, you can imagine, can't you! When I found out all the things Mrs Peters wanted me to learn and remember to do, I really did wet myself!

(But only a little bit, because I'd crossed my legs really tight!)

And I didn't tell anyone. Not even Gabby.

CHAPTER 12

After school finished that day, everyone ran across the playground really fast to tell their mums and dads who they were going to be, and what costumes they had to make!

Everyone was really smiley and excited. Except Liam Chaldecott's dad. When Liam told his dad he was an innkeeper and not a Joseph, his dad took him to the school office to complain.

Mum promised to make me the best Mary's helper outfit she could, but said she would definitely need Nanny's sewing machine to help her.

Gabby said if I had a blue dress, we would be matching! So Mum said she would see what she could do.

Then Gabby said it was all so exciting, we simply must play our

"I love Christmas!" game again – all the way home from school.

And guess what? There were still loads more lovely Christmassy things we could think of.

Plus Mum asked if she could join in our game too!

After we made her promise not to sing any more Christmas carols, we said she could.

"I love Christmas crackers!" said Gabby.

I said I loved Christmas crackers too, except the **trouble with Christmas crackers** is the toys inside them are too small.

Plus, if you pull the wrong end of the cracker off, you don't get a toy at all. Sometimes you don't get ANYTHING, or if you do, it's just a paper hat with a rubber band round it. Plus it's a paper hat that is only pretending to be a crown.

The **trouble with pretend crowns** is they're made of paper, not real crown.

If they were made of real crown like the ones a three king would wear, then they'd have real diamonds and jewels all over them! Plus they wouldn't rip if you had big hair like my Auntie Sue. Or big ears like my Uncle Clive.

"I love chocolate money!" I said. Except the **trouble with chocolate money** is you should be able to spend the wrappers.

I mean the wrappers on chocolate money look like real money, so why can't you spend them?

I wrapped the golden bits of my chocolate money around some shirt buttons once, and tried to spend them in a sweetshop. But it didn't work. The sweetshop owner said I could only buy sweets with real money.

That's the **trouble with sweet-shop owners**. They're really mean. Even at Christmas.

"I love robin redbreasts!" said Mum. (Which was much better than Christmas carols.)

"I love partridges in pear trees!" said Gabby.

The **trouble with partridges in pear trees** is I've never seen one.

I don't reckon Gabby has either. I like the sound of them, but there are never any partridges in my grampy's pear trees. Even on Christmas Days.

I've seen a blackbird in a pear tree, and a starling in a pear tree, and a sparrow and a blue tit quite near my grampy's pear trees, but I don't think there are any proper partridges anywhere near where I live.

"I love tangerines!" said Mum. Which was a bit naughty really, because it wasn't her go.

"I love party poppers!" I said.

"I love toboggans!" said Gabby.

"I love figs and dates!" said Mum, which was really naughty this time, because you weren't allowed to say two things at  once. Plus it wasn't even her game in the first place so if anyone was going to change the rules, it should have been me or Gabby, not my mum.

 "I love Christmas tinsel!" Gabby said. Then she changed it to Christmas biscuits.

The **trouble with Christmas biscuits** is in my house we're not allowed to open them until Christmas Day. Otherwise my mum says they won't be so special.

We always have a big box of special Christmas biscuits in our house every Christmas! They're much more special than normal biscuits (not including crunchy creams) because loads of them have got chocolate on, PLUS you get two whole layers of biscuits in one box!

How exciting is that! You can eat a whole great big layer, and then you can eat them all over again!

"I love nutcrackers!" said my mum. "And walnuts! And hazel nuts! And brazil nuts. And pecan nuts!"

Which was *five* things!

Which is three times worse than saying two things! So we banned

her from playing after that.

So THEN she started singing Christmas carols again ON PURPOSE!

All the way home again.

Honestly. Sometimes my mum can be SOOOOOOO not grown up!

CHAPTER 13

The next three weeks at school became so exciting we hardly had time to play our special "I love Christmas" game. Plus, once rehearsals for our school Christmas play started, we hardly did any proper lessons at all! Every morning after assembly Mrs Peters would divide us up into small groups, and then she would make us practise the words we would have to say to each other.

And then after lunch we would practise all the new songs we were going to have to sing in the play.

O Little Town of Baaaaaa-thlehem was my favourite song, but I wasn't allowed to learn that one, because I wasn't in the Woolly Wonkas.

Paula Potts was allowed to learn it because she was going to be the sheepdog and "sheepdog" has the word "sheep" in it. So that's all right probably.

But no one else was. (Although me and Gabby did learn some of the words in secret! Especially Baaaaaaaaaaaaaaaa-thlehem!!)

I was with Gabby for all my rehearsals, plus the three kings and

the shepherds joined us sometimes, to "gather round".

"Gather round" the manger is what Mrs Peters said everyone in the stable had to do once baby Jesus was born.

We didn't have a proper manger to gather round in rehearsals though, so we used a cardboard box instead.

It was quite a big box, and at first when Mrs Peters brought it into class one morning, it looked really exciting. But when I looked inside, it was EMPTY. There was no baby Jesus inside to "gather round" at all!

Then things got really exciting again.

After Mrs Peters had put the cardboard box on Gabby's desk, she clapped her hands and gave us the REALLY, REALLY brilliant news.

"Children," she said; "girls especially. This afternoon when you get home from school, I have a very special Christmas job for you all to do. After you've had your tea, or before you go to bed, I want you to look on the shelves in your bedroom, I want you to peer into your toyboxes or hunt through your toy cupboards and find me a dolly who you think might be special enough to be baby Jesus in the school Christmas play."

You can't imagine how quickly I crossed my legs after Mrs Peters said that! There was going to be a

SPECIAL dolly in the school Christmas play, and I was going to be the one who would be bathing and rocking and cradling it!

Then Mrs Peters said that if we had a special enough dolly at home we could bring it into school the next day!

I knew exactly which dolly I was going to bring in! And so did Gabby!!

And mine would be much better than Gabby's!

CHAPTER 14

The **trouble with Mrs Peters** is she's not very good at choosing baby Jesuses.

The dolly that Paula Potts brought into class the next day was really good, because it did real gurgling

Gurgle!

Gurgle!

sounds, and if you squeezed its arm it said, "I want my breakfast!"

Stephanie Brakespeare and Melanie Simpson both brought a really good dolly in too. It was called Baby Wee-Wee, and it had its own bottle filled with actual p r e t e n d milk that you could feed it. Plus it did real wees in its nappy afterwards!

I've wet my nappy!

425

Waaahh Waaahhhh!

Vicky Carrow's dolly did real tears and chuckling.

Nishta Baghwat's did wriggling and crawling. (Except sometimes it fell over and couldn't get up again.)

Shuffle! Shuffle!

Liberty
Pearce and
Collette Simpson
both brought
in a Baby
Dribble
Bibs.

BLERP!

ScreeEEeech!

Bernadette Laine brought
in a Baby First Tooth
that had glowing
red cheeks and
a temperature
checker!

427

Gabby's dolly was really, really good. It was called Baby Fidget Bottom, and when you sat it up it moved across the floor on its bottom! Plus its head turned, and its eyelids went up and down AND it made gurgling sounds and coochie-coo noises too!

But my dolly was the best dolly by far. My dolly was called Baby

Hiccups, and if you gave it water in a bottle to make the hiccups go away, it did really loud swallowing noises and then went, "HIC HIC HOORAY! MY HICCUPS HAVE STOPPED!"

How good is that!

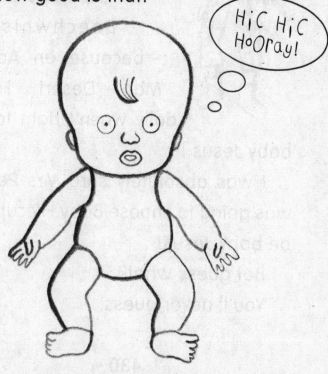

Eat bullets punk!

Mrs Peters said everyone in the class who had brought in a dolly had done really well. (Apart from Jack Beechwhistle, because an Action Man Desert Force dolly wasn't right to be baby Jesus.)

I was absolutely sure Mrs Peters was going to choose Baby Hiccups to be baby Jesus!

But guess what?

You'll never guess.

She didn't choose any of the exciting dollies at all!

She chose a really boring one!

Mrs Peters chose Laura Donnelly's dolly. And it wasn't called baby anything at all!

Laura Donnelly was really pleased, but when me and Gabby saw the dolly that Mrs Peters had chosen to be baby Jesus, we were really fed up.

After all, Gabby was the one who was going to get really tired giving birth to it, and I was the one who would have to get really busy helping her with it afterwards.

If you ask me, we were the ones

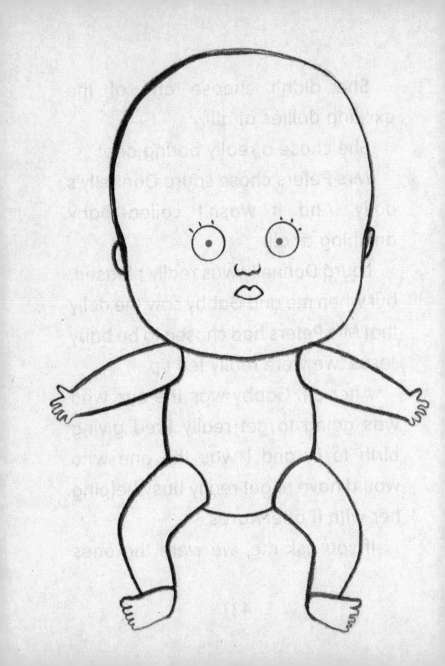

who should have chosen which dolly baby Jesus should be. Not Mrs Peters.

But Mrs Peters said that Laura Donnelly's dolly was perfect for the job.

Perfect for the job? It didn't gurgle, it didn't wee, it didn't chuckle, or crawl or fidget, or dribble or get nappy rash, and it definitely didn't get hiccups!!!

Laura Donnelly's dolly didn't have a bottle, or nappy cream, or a temperature checker! It didn't even have batteries!!!

Its eyes didn't move, its arms and legs didn't move. It wasn't special AT ALL!

WHICH WASN'T MY FAULT!!!!

When I told my mum at home time which dolly Mrs Peters had chosen to be baby Jesus, she stopped humming Christmas carols and said she was sure Mrs Peters had her reasons.

I asked my mum to go and complain to the school office about Laura Donnelly's dolly just like Liam

Chaldecott's dad had about Mrs Peters choosing the wrong Joseph.

But my mum said she wasn't the kind of parent who went into school offices complaining, even if Mrs Peters had picked the wrong dolly to be Jesus. She said being a teacher was a hard enough job as it was, without parents marching into school every day and moaning and groaning.

So I had no choice in the end.

If Laura Donnelly's dolly wasn't special, I just had to think of a way of MAKING IT SPECIAL!

CHAPTER 15

The **trouble with dollies that aren't special** is there is NO WAY they should be a baby Jesus dolly in a school Christmas play.

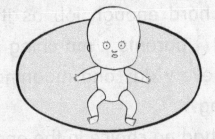

I mean, baby Jesus is the specialest most special baby in the world!

PLUS he's the son of GOD! And God is the specialest most special person

436

in the world. (Not including Santa.)

So there was no way a plain old boring dolly should have been a really special Jesus dolly in a school Christmas play.

Especially as I was the one who had been asked to behold him up for everyone to look at.

I mean, what were all the parents in the audience going to think when I behelded him up and he didn't look even the titchiest bit special?

If you were going to be a Mary's helper, you wouldn't want to behold up a baby Jesus who didn't look properly special, would you?

If you were a Mary's helper, you wouldn't even want to "gather round" a baby Jesus who didn't do things that were properly special, would you?

I bet if Santa made a baby Jesus dolly, he would make it do all sorts of properly special things. I bet he would make it laugh and gurgle and kick its legs, and cry and wet its nappy and everything. I bet a baby Jesus dolly made by Santa would have about twenty-seven batteries in it AT LEAST!

There's no way Santa would have wanted to gather round Laura Donnelly's baby Jesus dolly. Or behold it up.

Me and Gabby tried "gathering round" Laura Donnelly's dolly every day for THREE WHOLE WEEKS, but every time we looked into the cardboard box and did our rehearsing, all it did was LIE STILL!

It didn't even blink!

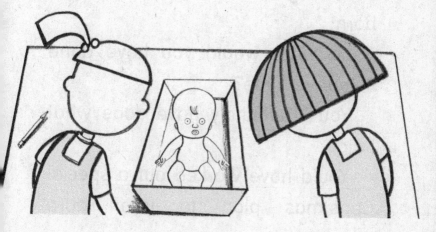

Mrs Peters said that newborn baby Jesuses weren't meant to do special things, and that Jesus would do more than enough special things when he grew up.

Trouble was, I wouldn't be beholding baby Jesus up when he was grown up. I would only be beholding him up when he was just born.

So what would you have done if you were me?

You'd definitely have done what I did.

You'd have worked out a special Christmas plan to turn Laura

Donnelly's boring dolly into a really special Jesus dolly, wouldn't you?

Especially if your best friend was going to be Mary in the school Christmas play and especially if Mary wanted her baby to look much more special too.

Our first plan would definitely have worked if Mrs Peters had let us do it. Our first plan was all Gabby's idea, and it was brilliant!

Why didn't I think of it! Paula Pott's mum had an actual real live actual baby at home! Plus he was an actual baby boy!! So instead of Laura Donnelly's useless dolly, why didn't we use him in our Christmas play!

He wasn't called Jesus, he was called Eric. . .

How special and exciting would that be!

Paula Potts was sure her mum would say yes.

Trouble was, Mrs Peters said no before we even got to ask!

She said having a real live baby Jesus in the school Christmas play was completely out of the question, and she was beginning to wonder whether putting me and Gabby together in the play was such a good idea after all.

So after that Gabby and me decided we would have to come up with a different Make Baby Jesus More Special Plan instead.

And this time we decided we wouldn't tell Mrs Peters about it, or anyone else at all!

CHAPTER 16

The **trouble with taking the batteries out of your mum's torch without asking** is when she goes to use it, the light inside the torch doesn't come on.

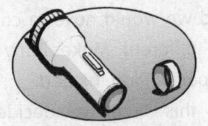

My mum was sure I'd taken the batteries out of her torch, but I crossed my fingers behind my back and said I hadn't.

The **trouble with taking the batteries out of the TV clicker without asking** is when someone turns the telly on, the telly doesn't come on at all. Neither do any of the programmes.

Gabby's mum and dad were sure Gabby had taken the batteries out of their TV clicker, but Gabby crossed her fingers behind her back too and said she hadn't as well.

That's the **trouble with doing secret plans**. You have to cross your fingers behind your back A LOT!

At first we thought we were going to get found out about the batteries, but when our mums got some new batteries, we knew they hadn't caught us and our secret plan was still working!

Or at least the first bit of it was.

For the second part of our Make Baby Jesus More Special Plan I had to ask my mum to sew big pockets into my Mary's helper cloak.

"Why does Mary's helper need big pockets?" my mum asked.

"To fit her camel and donkey food in," I fibbed. (I'd been rehearsing that answer as well as my other words too.)

Plus I had two lots of fingers crossed behind my back this time.

And guess what! My mum believed me! She really did sew big pockets into my costume. Which meant the second bit of our plan had worked as well!

All we had to do now was smuggle our stolen batteries into school.

The **trouble with smuggling stolen batteries into school** is you need a really good place to hide them.

At first we took them into school in our lunch boxes, but Mrs Baines, the dinner lady, saw them when I was having my yoghurt and made me tell her why they were there.

I told her I had an electric lunch box

and that the batteries were keeping my sandwiches fresh.

The **trouble with fibbing to Mrs Baines** is if you're eating your yoghurt, you don't have any fingers free to cross behind your back.

So Mrs Baines didn't believe me. She said that there were no such things as electric lunch boxes, and that she would keep the batteries in her pocket until after I'd finished my lunch.

Luckily she did give them back to me, otherwise part three of our Make Baby Jesus More Special Plan wouldn't have worked at all.

After that we had to hide our batteries somewhere else.

Gabby put her batteries in her pencil case because they were smaller than mine, but I put mine in my PE bag because I had four whoppers!

CHAPTER 17

When the curtains went back on the school stage this afternoon, we were all standing in our costumes and ready to start the play.

You should have seen how good everybody's costumes looked! I was wearing a blue robe with a golden rope belt round it, and on my head I had one of my nanny's best tea towels made into a Mary's helper hat.

Gabby was really excited too, especially as she was wearing her blue shoes. She had a blue robe with a blue belt and blue shawl and a blue hairband. Plus Mrs Peters had let her wear her own hair instead of a wig!

Nishta Baghwat had a golden crown with rubies stuck to it, Harry Bayliss's three king cloak had silver milk-bottle tops all over it, Daniel Carrington had a Joseph moustache to make him look older plus a wooden hammer to make him look like a real carpenter, Liberty Pearce had angel wings made out of real white goose feathers, Fiona Tucker didn't have feathers but she had six golden wings instead, plus a massive magic wand, the Roman soldiers all had real armour made out of tin foil, plus actual swords and cardboard daggers, and the Woolly Wonkas all had white T-shirts and cotton-wool balls stuck to their balaclavas!

Plus the clapping from the audience sounded really loud!

It was SOOOOOO EXCIIIITING!!!!!!!

I was standing on the stage behind a donkey, and couldn't see very much at first. That's the **trouble with donkey's ears**.

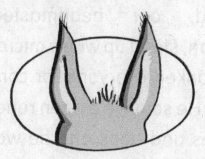

If you want to see between them you have to stand on tiptoe.

When I got up a bit higher, I could just about see my mum through the gap in between. She was sitting right in the front row of the audience next to Gabby's mum and dad. I don't think they could see us, but we still gave them a really big wave.

Once the clapping had nearly stopped, our headmaster, Mr Sturgeon, stood up with a microphone and thanked everyone for coming to see us. He said we'd been rehearsing for ages and ages and he was sure we would put on a very good Christmas show.

Then he thanked all the teachers for rehearsing us, then he thanked Mr Benedict for playing the piano, then he told everyone how to get out of the school hall if there was a fire, then he said that if mums or dads wanted to take photographs or make films of us, they weren't allowed, and then he said our school Christmas bazaar would be on Saturday, and then he said he needed more helpers to help, and then his microphone stopped working so we couldn't hear what he was saying, and then the microphone started working again, and then he said that after the play had finished, the school was collecting money for the NSPCC, and then he sat down.

That's the **trouble with headmasters**. They do go on a bit.

While everyone in the audience was clapping and thanking our headmaster for sitting down, the curtains on the stage closed, and Mrs Peters told us all to go and stand in our special places.

My special place was right over to one side, behind Daniel McNichol.

Then Miss Leames turned off all the lights in the assembly hall, and everything went dark! It went so dark everyone started giggling, because it was so exciting!

Then the angels started to sing the first song, the lights came on, the curtains opened again, and GUESS WHAT . . . Gabby had to walk onto the stage all by herself!!!!!

She wasn't shy or anything. In fact before she told everyone how poor her and Joseph were, she waved with BOTH hands to her mum and dad!

Gabby looked like a really good Mary. In fact everyone looked good. Nishta looked good, Bernadette looked good, even Jack Beechwhistle looked good!

If only baby Jesus had looked good too.

Then everything wouldn't have gone so wrong.

CHAPTER 18

The **trouble with secret winks** is you have to be careful Mrs Peters doesn't see you do them. Especially if you're doing acting in a school Christmas play.

Mrs Peters kept doing loads of normal winks every time someone remembered their words or did their acting right.

But Gabby's and my secret winks were far more secret than that.

Gabby did her first secret wink to me just after she got on her cardboard donkey to go to Baaaaaaaaaa-thlehem.

Secret winks mean *Get ready to do our secret plan!* I was absolutely ready and everything!

In fact I was so so EXCITED, the tea towel on my head had started to wobble. I'd learned all my words off by heart. I'd been practising them after school, and in the bath, and even on the loo!

"BEHOLD THE KING OF KINGS IS BORN!"

That's what I was going to say, in my loudest Mary's helper voice.

I knew exactly what else I had to do too. Plus I had all the batteries in my pocket to do it!!!!!!

All I had to do now was wait for secret wink number two.

And find a better place to see Gabby.

The **trouble with big shining stars** is they stick up like donkey's ears too.

Especially if Daniel McNicholl is holding the pole and waving it in front of your face.

In the end I had to whisper to tell him to lean the pole on his other shoulder, otherwise I would miss my second secret wink.

Gabby and me had five secret

winks planned.

Gabby gave me her second wink when she arrived at the Inn with Joseph.

Our third secret wink would be when the innkeeper took them to the stable.

The fourth secret wink would be when baby Jesus was born in the manger.

And the fifth and most special secret wink would be when she handed baby Jesus to me to take away!

After that, everything would be down to me . . .

CHAPTER 19

The **trouble with waiting for secret winks** is it's worse than waiting for Christmas!

I was almost nearly wetting myself by the third secret wink.

My tea towel was almost falling off my head by the fourth secret wink.

And I was nearly fainting with excitement by the fifth one! Everything was going so well!

Everyone was remembering their lines really well, Except Daniel Carrington. He was too busy playing with his hammer.

Luckily Mrs Peters had learned to say Joseph's lines for him. Otherwise

Daniel and Gabby would never even have got to Bethlehem. They probably wouldn't even have left Nazareth.

Luckily Mrs Peters had learned absolutely everybody's lines for them, so when anyone forgot their words, she said them for them.

She didn't need to say any of my words for me though. I'd learned every single one of my seven words! Trouble is, I wouldn't actually get a chance to say them all.

I would get to say most of them.

I would get to say "BEHOLD".

And I would get to say "THE".

And I would even get to say "KING OF KINGS . . ."

But I wouldn't have time to say "IS BORN" because by the time I'd got to the "IS BORN" bit, everything in our secret Make Baby Jesus More Special Plan, started to go wrong . . .

REALLY WRONG actually.

As in REALLY, REALLY, REALLY, REALLY WRONG . . .

WHICH WASN'T MY FAULT!

CHAPTER 20

The **trouble with having to wait so long for a fifth secret wink** is my heartbeat nearly jumped out of my ears when it happened!

At first, everything in our secret plan looked like it was going to work.

I actually walked out onto the stage really well. I actually took baby

Jesus from Gabby really brilliantly. I actually cradled him in my arms really brilliantly too. I even actually managed to do a really big wink to  my mum before it all went dark on the stage and the Woolly Wonkas started to sing.

It was when I got Laura Donnelly's dolly behind the curtains that it all started to go wrong.

That was when I first realized my batteries had nowhere to go in.

That was our special plan, you see.

To put lots of new batteries into

 Laura Donnelly's dolly.

Except Laura Donnelly's dolly didn't have a place for new batteries.

Because Laura Donnelly's dolly had never come with batteries in the first place.

The **trouble with dollies that never came with batteries in the first place** is it's really hard to fit new batteries in.

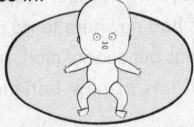

When I turned Laura Donnelly's dolly over and lifted up his clothes, I thought it would have a special place in his back where I could fit some batteries in. Or maybe in his tummy.

All the dollies that everyone else brought into class had special places for batteries. But Laura Donnelly's dolly didn't have any places like that at all.

The **trouble with not having any places like that at all** is it makes you go all hot.

Especially if you have extra big pockets in your Mary's helper outfit full of batteries that need to go in.

And double especially if the Woolly Wonkas have nearly finished singing *O Little Town of Baaaaaathlehem* and it's almost time for you to go back on stage and behold a special baby Jesus up for everyone to see.

So I panicked.

The **trouble with panicking** is it makes you do things you really shouldn't do.

Like trying to MAKE a place inside Laura Donnelly's dolly for your batteries to go.

At first I only pulled her dolly's head a little bit.

But then I pulled it a bit hard.

The **trouble with pulling the head of Laura Donnelly's dolly a bit hard** is it makes it come off in your hand.

Which was handy at first, because it meant I could poke about six of my batteries into his tummy.

Trouble was, then I couldn't get the head to go back on.

Double trouble was, then the Woolly Wonkas did stop singing.

Triple trouble was, then the lights on the stage came back on and everyone was waiting for me to come back to the manger and behold the baby Jesus up!

So I tried my best.

I tried my really hardest.

I pushed as many batteries into the dolly's tummy as I could, and then I really, really, honestly tried to get his head to go back on.

But however hard I pushed, and however much I twisted, it wouldn't stay on at all.

So I had to put my hand behind his head and hold it there instead.

Trouble was, I still hadn't taken him back to Mary, and I still hadn't behelded him up.

The **trouble with beholding up a dolly with a wobbly head** is when you lift him up to say "Behold the king of kings" . . .

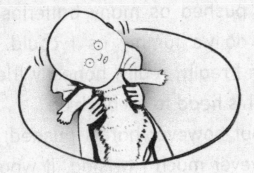

. . . . the head falls out of the blanket.

The **trouble with a head falling out of a blanket** is it makes you try and catch it before it reaches the floor. Plus it makes Laura Donnelly scream really loudly.

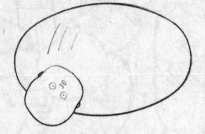

The **trouble with trying to catch a dolly's head before it reaches the floor** is it makes you drop the rest of the dolly too.

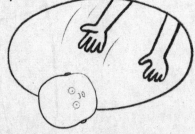

The **trouble with dropping the rest of the dolly** is the batteries fall out of his tummy and bounce across the floor.

The **trouble with batteries bouncing across the floor** is then Mary tries to help too.

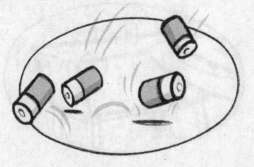

The **trouble with Mary trying to help** is the batteries will make her skid. Especially if she's wearing blue shoes.

The **trouble with Mary skidding** is she will try to grab hold of the manger.

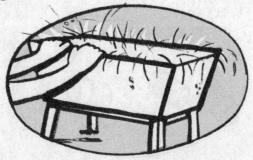

The **trouble with grabbing hold of the manger** is the manger will crash onto the floor.

The **trouble with the manger crashing to the floor** is the three kings will jump out of the way.

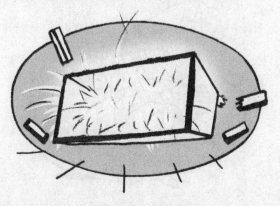

The **trouble with the three kings jumping out of the way** is they will come down and land on the batteries too.

The **trouble with the three kings landing on the batteries too** is it means they will skid into the shepherds.

The **trouble with skidding into the shepherds** is the shepherds will trip over the angels.

The **trouble with tripping over the angels** is the angels will crash into the Woolly Wonkas.

The **trouble with crashing into the Woolly Wonkas** is the Woolly Wonkas will charge into Mrs Peters.

The **trouble with charging into Mrs Peters** is Mrs Peters will grab hold of the stage curtains.

The **trouble with grabbing hold of the stage curtains** is then all the stage curtains will fall down.

Which makes everyone in the audience jump out of their seats. And Mrs Leames faint.

And Joseph's moustache drop off.

And the shining star snap in the middle.

Which wasn't really my plan.

But I suppose . . . was kind of actually my fault. Because I was the one who did the batteries. Not Gabby.

When Mrs Peters untangled herself from the curtains, she was so cross she couldn't speak.

Paula Potts was howling like a wolf instead of a sheepdog.

Jack Beechwhistle had gone berserk with a cardboard sword because he hadn't had the chance to set his soldiers on anyone.

And our headmaster had gone a funny purple colour all over his face.

Then, after that, the story of Christmas sort of ended.

And the story of me being told off kind of began.

CHAPTER 21

"MUUUUUMMMM!!!!"

"YES, DAISY."

"CAN I COME OUT OF MY BEDROOM YET?"

"NO, YOU CAN'T, DAISY. YOU'RE IN DISGRACE!"

Told you. I told you I was in big trouble. I bet Gabby's been sent to her bedroom too.

"MUUUUUUUUMMMMM!!!!!"

"WHAT NOW, DAISY?"

"Can we have a bonfire in the garden this evening?"

"No, we can't."

"PLEEEAAAAAAASSSSSSSE, MUM. IT'S REALLY, REALLY IMPORTANT."

"Why, Daisy? Exactly why is it really, really important?"

"NO REASON."

"No reason is no reason to have a bonfire then, is it, Daisy?"

"ER . . . I NEED TO SEND ANOTHER LETTER TO SANTA . . ."

498

To Santa
Santa's House
The North Pole

Dear Santa

I don't know if you saw what happened at the school Christmas play this afternoon, but if you did, please don't be cross.

My mum says that you see everything, and that if you see children doing something wrong then you won't bring them any presents on Christmas Eve. My mum says you put coal in their stockings instead.

The trouble with coal is I don't really like it very much. Plus we haven't got a fire it can go on. We've only got radiators.

Double plus what happened in the school Christmas play today

wasn't totally really my fault.
It was only sort of really my
fault.
Mostly, it was Christmas's fault.
It was Christmas's fault for
making me SOOOOOOO
EXCITED. I've been excited since
September so that proves it's
Christmas's fault.
My mum says I always get into
trouble when I get excited.
So pleeeeease don't be cross with
me, because Christmas is the most
exciting time of the year!
Plus, if you put coal in my
stocking then you should
definitely put coal in Mrs Peters'
stocking too.
If Mrs Peters had chosen a
special dolly to be baby
Jesus instead of one with no
batteries, then Gabby and me

wouldn't have needed to have
a secret plan in the first place.
Or do secret winks.
All we were trying to do was
make our baby Jesus more
special. Because baby Jesus
is the most special baby in all
the world.
That's why I had to put
batteries in him.
Which is why I had to take
his head off.
So I could get the batteries in.
I know our secret plan didn't
work, and I know I spoiled
the Christmas play for everyone,
especially Laura Donnelly and
Jack Beechwhistle, and I suppose
Mrs Peters too, but I have been
good for the rest of the year,
Santa. (Not including the other
times I've got into trouble.)

So please, Santa, PLEASE can
I have presents in my stocking
on Christmas Day, and not
horrible bits of coal?
I promise I won't be naughty
ever again, plus I will do you
a really, really good deal.
My deal is if you give me the
presents that I wrote down on
my Christmas list, I will come
and work for you for free when
I'm seventeen!
I'll bring my own red scissors,
I'll wrap presents and
make toys and feed ALL
the reindeers, and I'll work
harder than all the other elves
who help you. Plus, if you want
me to be more elfy, I'll even
paint myself green!
I hope you like this deal,
Santa. Because I really want

a bike that fires torpedoes.
I love you lots and lots
and LOTS, Santa. Christmas
is my most favourite time of
the year EVER! So pleeeeease
don't be cross with me.
Enough people are cross
with me already.
Happy Christmas. I hope
you get this letter, Santa.

Love,
Daisy

PS. Gabby says, do you make
underwater helicopters too?

to Santa

DAISY'S
TROUBLE
INDEX

The trouble with . . .

Pulling the head of Laura Donnelly's dolly a bit too hard 480

 Beholding up a dolly with a wobbly head 482

 A head falling out of a blanket 484

 Trying to catch a dolly's head before it reaches the floor 484

 Dropping the rest of the dolly 485

 Batteries bouncing across the floor 485

Daisy's Burglar Quiz

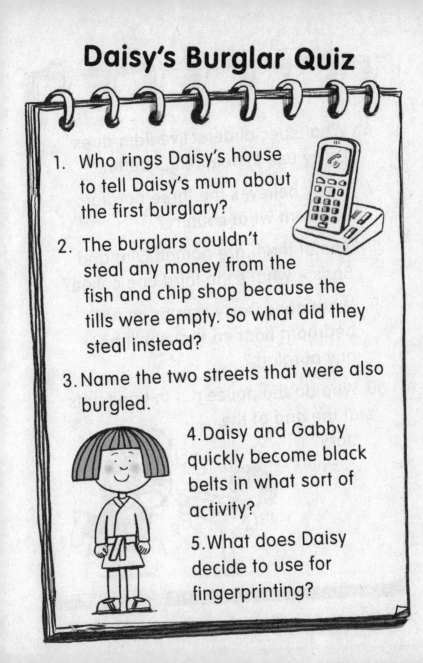

1. Who rings Daisy's house to tell Daisy's mum about the first burglary?

2. The burglars couldn't steal any money from the fish and chip shop because the tills were empty. So what did they steal instead?

3. Name the two streets that were also burgled.

4. Daisy and Gabby quickly become black belts in what sort of activity?

5. What does Daisy decide to use for fingerprinting?

6. What special detective item does Daisy use to see things better?

7. Daisy believes the three burglars are from what country?

8. Two of them are named Olaf and Boris – what's the third one called?

9. What does Daisy scatter on her bedroom floor so that she'll hear any burglars?

10. Who do the police put in handcuffs at the end of the story?

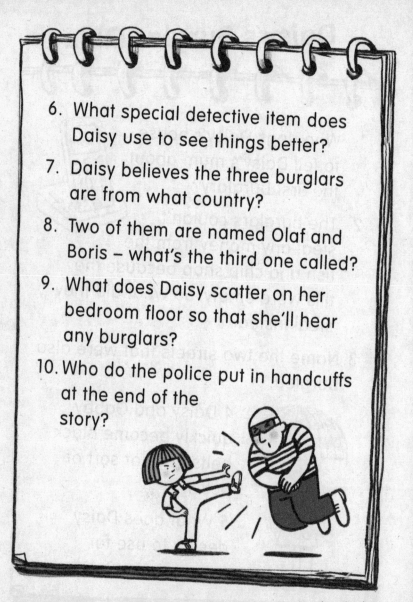

Daisy's Christmas Quiz

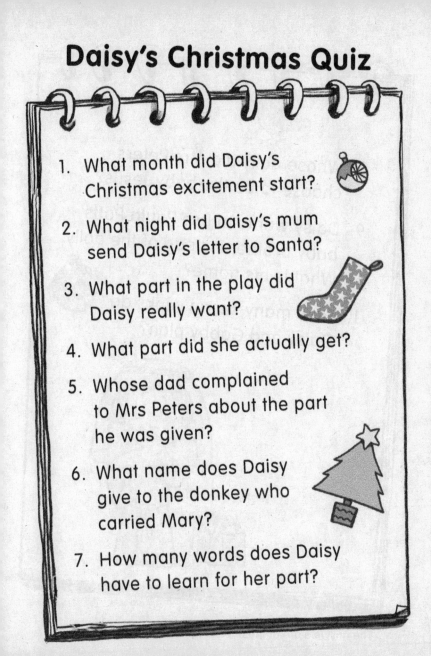

1. What month did Daisy's Christmas excitement start?

2. What night did Daisy's mum send Daisy's letter to Santa?

3. What part in the play did Daisy really want?

4. What part did she actually get?

5. Whose dad complained to Mrs Peters about the part he was given?

6. What name does Daisy give to the donkey who carried Mary?

7. How many words does Daisy have to learn for her part?

8. Whose dolly did Mrs Peters choose to be the baby Jesus?

9. Daisy wants to use Paula Potts' baby brother instead of the dolly. What is his name?

10. How many secret winks do Daisy and Gabby plan?

Detective Facts

Did you know . . .

- One of the most famous detectives of all time was Sherlock Holmes. He was created by a writer called Sir Arthur Conan Doyle, and he had a trusty sidekick called Dr John Watson. Sherlock Holmes lived at a house in Baker Street, London.

- Another famous detective was Miss Marple, who appeared in lots of mystery books by Agatha Christie. This character has been played by twelve different actresses over the years!

- When a crime scene is investigated for clues like fingerprints, this is called forensics. Other things that you might look for at a crime scene include footprints, hairs or threads from clothing, tyre tracks, handwriting or broken glass.

- Witnesses are very important at a crime scene. This means anyone who might have seen the crime happen, or might have spotted the criminal doing anything suspicious.

- You can test how good a witness your friends or family would be by asking them to look at a photograph of some people – for example, in a newspaper – for one minute. Then take the photograph away and ask them questions about it. How many people were in it? Who was the tallest? Was anyone wearing a hat, or jewellery? See how many things they remember correctly!

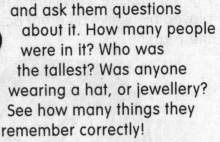

Match them up!

Can you match all the children in Daisy's class to the parts they played in the Christmas play?

Gabby ....

Jack Beechwhistle ....

Vicky Carrow ....

Nishta Baghwat ....

Daniel Carrington ....

Liberty Pearce ....

Daniel McNicholl ....

Liam Chaldecott ....

Paula Potts ....

David Alexander ....

Colin Kettle ....

Melanie Simpson ....

Harry Bayliss ....

Angel • Barmaid • Sheepdog • Mary
• Joseph • Innkeeper • Shepherd •
Three king with the gold • Three king
with the frankincense • Three king
with the myrrh • A bright shining star
• King Herod • A Roman soldier

Daisy's Wordsearch

Can you find these words in the wordsearch below?

- Fish
- Chips
- Clue
- Detective
- Ransom Note
- Police
- Prison
- Crime
- Doritos
- Prints
- Handcuffs

h	s	i	f	h	k	a	e	c	s	r	m	c
n	d	k	a	c	m	r	k	l	g	k	b	h
b	l	s	b	t	c	a	t	u	a	d	h	i
d	e	t	e	c	t	i	v	e	a	b	k	p
f	c	a	m	a	c	j	m	x	e	w	i	s
d	i	a	s	o	r	g	l	t	b	e	s	x
s	l	r	t	j	w	t	o	f	g	h	o	z
t	o	t	p	h	a	n	d	c	u	f	f	s
n	p	j	r	x	m	a	t	r	r	s	l	f
i	m	a	i	o	o	b	i	i	w	t	h	j
r	b	n	s	n	s	l	l	m	o	b	e	i
p	r	n	o	g	p	a	r	e	n	a	t	b
m	a	s	n	w	l	r	j	b	b	l	h	m
r	d	c	l	e	m	s	o	t	i	r	o	d

Gabby's Mince Pies

Gabby loves mince pies at Christmas! Here's a recipe for them – make sure you ask a grown-up for help.

You'll need:

225g cold butter, chopped into little cubes

350g plain flour

100g golden caster sugar

A pinch of salt

250g mincemeat

1 small egg

Icing sugar

What to do:

1. To make the pastry, rub the butter into the flour with your fingertips.

2. Then add the golden caster sugar and a pinch of salt.

3. Scoop up the pastry mixture into a ball and give it a quick knead with your hands. It will feel quite firm.

4. Preheat the oven to 200°C.

5. Take two 12-hole baking trays. Roll out 24 small lumps of pastry, each about the size of a walnut. Put each lump into a hole and press it down, so that the pastry lines the bottom and the sides.

6. Spoon mincemeat into each hole.

7. Roll out the rest of the pastry with a rolling pin, and use a star-shaped pastry cutter to cut out a lid for each pie. Carefully put the lids on the pies and gently press down to seal them in place.

8. Beat 1 small egg and brush a small amount of egg on the tops of the pies.

9. Bake in the oven for 20 minutes until golden.

10. Leave to cool in the tin for 5 minutes, then remove to a wire rack to cool fully. Dust with icing sugar before serving and eating!

Daisy's Detective Checklist

What important things do you think
Daisy needs to be a detective?

Daisy's Clues

Can you remember the first eight clues Daisy and Gabby collected on Daisy's street?

1. _____

2. _____

3. _____

4. _____

5. _____

6. _____

7. _____

8. _____

Imagine what other clues you might find on your own street!

9. _____

10. _____

11. _____

12. _____

13. _____

14. _____

15. _____

16. _____

If you can't get to sleep on Christmas Eve . . .

Try counting sheep. If that doesn't work, try counting reindeer. If that doesn't work, try counting snowmen. If that doesn't work, try counting robins. If that doesn't work, try counting mince pies with legs.

If that doesn't work, try counting the mince pie crumbs in Santa's beard.

Have you read these other Daisy books?

Have you read these other Daisy books?

Answers

Daisy's Christmas Quiz:

1. September
2. Bonfire Night
3. The three kings with the gold
4. Mary's helper
5. Liam Chaldecott
6. Buttons
7. Seven
8. Laura Donnelly
9. Eric
10. Five

Daisy's Burglars Quiz:

1. Grampy
2. Some big bags of frozen cods and haddocks
3. Holly Way and Cypress Drive
4. Burglar fu
5. Icing sugar
6. Magnifying glass
7. Russia
8. Igor
9. Doritos
10. Mrs Pike

Match them up

Gabby	Mary
Jack Beechwhistle	King Herod
Vicky Carrow	The three king with the frankincense
Nishta Baghwat	The three king with the gold
Daniel Carrington	Joseph
Liberty Pearce	Angel
Daniel McNicholl	A bright shining star
Liam Chaldecott	Innkeeper
Paula Potts	Sheepdog
David Alexander	Shepherd
Colin Kettle	A Roman soldier
Melanie Simpson	Barmaid
Harry Bayliss	The three king with the myrrh

Daisy's Clues

1. A piece of chewed-up chewing gum
2. A little piece of metal
3. A piece of dirty paper
4. A piece of string
5. A half-sucked Polo mint
6. Some suspicious leaves
7. A burglar's glove
8. Some dandruff

Daisy's Wordsearch